"You're Dangerous to Me, Sarah Lynn Abbot," He Whispered.

"Dangerous and addictive. Do you know that I want you? I could hardly keep my hands off you in Athens. I couldn't get enough of looking at you."

"I didn't think you noticed me at all at first. I thought you were looking for someone else. Another woman." Her lips met each foray of his between the words they spoke.

Sighing, he released her. His smile was filled with an irony she didn't comprehend. "No, it was you I was looking for. It was always you," he added on a deeply serious note that seemed to relate to some time other than the recent past.

LAURIE PAIGE

was born on a farm in Kentucky, the youngest of seven children. She and her husband worked their way through college, and she draws on these experiences as well as those of working as a reliability and data systems engineer on the Space Shuttle for her heroines.

Dear Reader:

SILHOUETTE DESIRE is an exciting new line of contemporary romances from Silhouette Books. During the past year, many Silhouette readers have written in telling us what other types of stories they'd like to read from Silhouette, and we've kept these comments and suggestions in mind in developing SILHOUETTE DESIRE.

DESIREs feature all of the elements you like to see in a romance, plus a more sensual, provocative story. So if you want to experience all the excitement, passion and joy of falling in love, then SILHOUETTE DESIRE is for you.

Karen Solem
Editor-in-Chief
Silhouette Books

LAURIE PAIGE
Journey To Desire

Silhouette Desire

Published by Silhouette Books New York

America's Publisher of Contemporary Romance

Silhouette Books by Laurie Paige

Gypsy Enchantment (DES #123)
South of the Sun (ROM #296)
Lover's Choice (SE #170)
A Tangle of Rainbows (ROM #333)
Journey to Desire (DES #195)

SILHOUETTE BOOKS
300 E. 42nd St., New York, N.Y. 10017

ISBN: 0-373-05195-6

First Silhouette Books printing March, 1985

10 9 8 7 6 5 4 3 2 1

America's Publisher of Contemporary Romance

Printed in the U.S.A.

**Journey
To Desire**

1

Greece was more than a place; it was a state of mind.

Freedom, thought Sarah Lynn Abbot as she stood on the tiny balcony of her hotel room, her eyes roaming with an almost nostalgic gleam over Athens. Freedom. And yet it was more than that.

Engineering, science, mathematics—all began in Athens. So did theater, poetry, and medicine. Philosophy got its start in Delphi. The philosophy of sports—including those American favorites, football and baseball—was born in the games at Olympia.

The most basic tenets of Western civilization and, therefore, of herself, came from here. This knowledge reached inside her spirit and touched a resonant chord. It was as if she had returned to the place of her birth.

She smiled wryly as she drew a deep breath. Another thing she'd noticed was that the air in a city smelled the same whether in Greece or the States . . . polluted!

This was her third day in Athens since returning from a five-day sight-seeing trip through the country. She had done all the things tourists did in the city: viewed the Acropolis, the Agora, the National Museum; nibbled cheese and sipped wine at the Plaka while listening to the bouzouki music; visited all the shops. Tonight she was going to the Sound and Light show.

Turning from the view of the Parthenon in the moonlight, she automatically recalled that the temple had been built for Athena. She also remembered that the Greek word *parthenos* meant virgin and was a root of the scientific word *parthenogenesis,* a term referring to the development of an unfertilized cell—a "virgin birth." Grinning to herself, she admitted that if she ever had kids, that was the way she would probably have to get them.

In twenty-five years and eight months of living, she had never had what she considered a real date, one in which the man liked her personality, her mind, and her looks. Faced with her formidable intelligence, most men were either struck dumb with awe or envy, after which they turned to less threatening females, or they wanted to use her talents for their own gain or pet project.

The look of amusement left her face, and lips that were incredibly soft but had rarely been kissed parted on another sigh as she picked up her sweater and left the pleasant room. For almost a year, she had planned her big escape, and now that she had accomplished her goal, something was still missing.

Or someone, she thought a few minutes later, walking behind a couple who strolled hand in hand to Pynx, the theater on the little hill beside the Acropolis. She bought an eighty-drachma seat and settled herself on the hard bench to watch the show, which would begin at nine o'clock. The voices around her were mostly British and German with a liberal sprinkling of good old down-home American thrown in. A few Orientals dotted the crowd.

She saw the couple she'd followed over sitting three rows down. The man's arm was protectively laid over the woman's shoulders. A startling smart of tears made her look quickly away.

Her brown eyes fell on a figure that was familiar, and the nostalgic smile curved the soft lips again. She had seen so many of the same people at the tourist places that they seemed like old friends.

Observing the tall man she had noticed at the museums and ruins yesterday and today, she thought he was an American—for no reason other than the fact that he was about six feet tall and rather brawny, maybe a hundred and eighty pounds, with good shoulders and arms.

Not to mention thighs and hips, she laughed silently. And his face wasn't bad, either. Actually she thought he was good-looking. Watch it, old girl, she warned herself sternly.

For the past five years, she had considered herself ripe for an affair and had guarded her heart against succumbing to puerile emotions. Which seemed rather ironic, looking back on her life.

The plain truth of the matter was that she hadn't been tempted by a man since a classmate in college had taken her out several times and then tried to get her to let him copy all her lab reports. She had been sixteen or seventeen at the time and terribly idealistic . . . and terribly in love.

All the men she associated with now were twenty to forty years her senior, just as they had been most of her life. When she had moved to a suburb of Washington, D.C., and gone to work, had she harbored a tiny hope that there, at last, she might meet someone who would love her for herself?

The lights around the stage area came on, and the music began. In English, they were told the history of the sites that were illuminated. Sarah forgot about the man who stood casually at the back of the audience, watching over the crowd.

For forty-five minutes, she was lost in a world of ancient wonder that should have been hers. Although she, a woman, would never have been admitted to their inner circles, she felt more at home with the thoughts of those long-dead people than with those of her own generation.

When she rose to leave, the now-familiar couple was once again ahead of her. The man's hand rested on the curve of the woman's hip and his fingers caressed the flesh beneath the loose blouse she wore.

Sarah had no doubts about what they would be doing when they got back to their hotel room. She smiled, but then the smile went crooked and disappeared. A strange ache filled her chest, causing her to step aside and let the crowd precede her.

Standing there, she considered her sudden emotion. She didn't understand herself anymore. She was restless and tearful instead of ecstatically happy about being on her long-awaited and hard-earned vacation. Really, she thought, irritated with her reactions.

Then the flare of a lighter caught her attention.

Standing a short distance from her was the American. As he raised the flame to his cigarette, she noticed a scar on his wrist and knew a brief, sympathetic pain for him. The wound had been long and deep.

He released the lever and the light went out before she could get more than a glimpse of the cleanly molded lips pressed around the filter tip. He replaced the device in his pocket, pushing it down into his tight jeans with his thumb.

She wondered how one went about the task of picking up a man. Could she walk up and say "Hi, there!" in a bright voice as if she knew what she were doing?

He glanced over at her, and her breath stirred fitfully in her chest. He smiled in a reassuring manner that was in no way a come-on, then he looked away, toward the backs of the departing audience. He made no move toward her, nor did he acknowledge her presence in any other way.

She experienced a stab of hurt disappointment that he wasn't interested enough to speak or fall into step beside her. *Old gal, you are turning into a desperate old maid,* she scolded as she hurried after the crowd. Turning once, she saw him strolling at a leisurely pace, his step long and sure, along the street where her hotel was located. Maybe he was staying at the same place.

Suppressing that hopeful thought, she returned to her room, only to stand gazing up at the Doric structure of the Parthenon until the hour was very late. Then she went to bed.

Sweat glistened lightly on the coppery smoothness of tanned forearms as Mark Terrington stood in front of a shop window perusing the display of items behind the glass. The May breeze was pleasant if one stayed in the shade, but he was standing in direct sunlight. His eyes squinted against the sun's rays as he glanced up, observing the traffic along the street with a curiously alert gaze that was belied by the easy movement of his powerful shoulders as he turned and started down the sidewalk. He seemed to be in no hurry; only his glance shifted quickly, running along the storefronts ahead to a position in front of an open shoe stall.

He hadn't slept well last night. And he knew why. His seemingly casual glance flicked over the people hurrying through the shopping district and came to rest briefly on the girl. His expression turned slightly grim.

He shook his head impatiently as he experienced a return of the restlessness that had penetrated his slumber the previous night. He had been tempted to seek consolation with one of the available women on the street, but, after the girl, the thought had been repugnant to him. "Idealistic fool," he muttered to himself.

Most men wouldn't admit it, but one of the major reasons they visited brothels was just to receive the touch of another human, the feel of a warm body in the night to make them think they weren't alone . . . when they actually were.

A touch of humanness, he thought, and his eyes were drawn back to the shoe stall and the girl. To have a girl like that . . .

His lips pulled tightly against his teeth as his anger with himself and his wandering thoughts grew. Discipline was the first rule of this game. In ten years, he had learned that well.

He forced his mind back to the problem at hand. He still hadn't recovered from his shock two days ago when he'd realized that the girl and the genius he was supposed to find were the same person. It just didn't seem possible.

Was she trying to defect? The psychologist who had guided and charted her life since she had been brought to him as a precocious four-year-old by her worried parents said she wasn't.

The Brain, as he had thought of her until he'd actually seen her, had grown up in Raleigh, North Carolina, near Duke University. The Research Triangle was the general name given to the area because of the multitude of colleges and big businesses in that section of the state.

Mark had a sudden vision of her as a child, serious in demeanor, playing with an abacus while her anxious parents consulted with a cadre of experts headed by Dr.

Fielding, the psychologist, on how to raise her. He felt sorry for Sarah Lynn Abbot, child prodigy.

He remembered his own youth in Indiana, the demands his parents had made on him, the treachery and infidelity they'd practiced until, disgusted, he had left home at twenty-one to find his own place in the world, rejecting his parents' world of idle wealth. Was he any better off now? he wondered. His pity for Sarah Abbot extended to himself.

Well, hell, Terrington, he silently mocked, why don't you go buy a beer so you can cry in it?

Walking on down the street, he paused near the place where she was trying on leather sandals as if he had nothing better to do than look idly around.

One reason he had been asked to take this job was because he had a remarkable memory for faces. Ironically the man in the State Department hadn't been able to supply him with a really good photo of the genius.

There was no high school graduation picture of Sarah Abbot—for the simple reason that she hadn't graduated. At fifteen, she had been moved to Duke University under the auspices of Dr. Fielding. By the time she was twenty-one, she had a Ph.D. in math. Now she was a cryptologist working in the Pentagon for the military and living in a large high-security apartment building on the Virginia side of the Potomac River.

The military could use some brains, he thought, and his lips curled into a smile of admiration as he recalled how she had escaped the net of protection that was always around her. It was only by intimidating her best friend that they had been able to find out where the Brain was heading—and that was toward a cruise on a cargo ship in the Greek Isles.

As soon as the department discovered her plans, they had acted to place one of their men aboard the ship as a deckhand. Mark was to look for her in Athens, gain her

13

confidence, and go on the freighter cruise with her as a passenger. So far, so good. He had found her; now he had to strike up a friendship.

Greece seemed an appropriate destination for a person in her line of work. *Kryptos* meant "hidden" in Greek. Sarah Abbot solved secret codes and ciphers, cracking one in a few months that the Pentagon had thought would take years to decipher with a computer working full-time. That must have blown their minds. He chuckled, wondering what she did in her spare time. Solved those brain-teaser puzzles, he assumed.

When he had first spotted Sarah Lynn Abbot, girl genius, in a museum the other day, he had thought she was a teenager, about seventeen years old, until she had turned so he could see her face. Then he had been stunned as realization dawned that here was the Brain.

Jolting himself out of his memories and back to the present, he quickly surveyed the whole area before ambling closer. She was wearing a pair of tan jeans that hugged her fanny in an alluring manner as she bent forward to fasten the sandals she was considering.

The man in the booth said something to her, touching the shoe and making expansive motions with his hands. Both she and the shoe salesman laughed then, the sound rolling along the street, reaching Mark and making him envious. He wanted to be the one who made her laugh.

All of a sudden he wished that he were twenty-one again and she were a seventeen-year-old girl on the brink of womanhood and that they were going away together to start a new life in a new world.

Fool, he thought with swift, bitter remorse. He had never been as innocent as she looked, not with his family's friends around to clue him in to the mysteries of life. He had been fifteen at the time of his initiation.

The girl continued talking to the sidewalk salesman, each using a lot of sign language and laughter. She obviously didn't speak Greek. Mark was aware of the moment she straightened, apparently deciding to buy the sandals, and then paid the merchant. She turned toward him. His insides tightened, and he felt an ache in his loins.

Down, boy, he rebuked his body and his emotions at the same time. The next thing he knew, he'd be running after her, begging for a date like a school kid. He was supposed to appear to be a successful businessman who hadn't had a vacation in years and was tired of it all.

Upon seeing him, she stopped, and as he watched her he wondered about her youth. He remembered his own, which had been lonely. His parents had brought him to Greece once. They had mostly stayed by the pool at the hotel, drinks in hand, complaining about the heat or the prices or the other rich tourists who didn't give a damn about the places they visited.

He shook off his sudden anger with his own parents and with hers. That was in the past. He smiled in a friendly way, trying not to let the desire that still taunted him show in his gaze. Her eyes became questioning as he continued to look at her. She seemed so damned young and innocent, so sparkling with life as she walked toward him. He wanted her, he realized—in every way a man could want a woman.

Her hair was in a mass of curls, totally unlike the way it had been in the picture of her. There it had been scraped back into a ponytail. Neither was she wearing the large oval-framed glasses as pictured. Her eyes were an even medium brown like a piece of velvet.

He pulled his eyes from her to scan the street and store-fronts, noting every detail of change since the last time he had looked. There was a face in a taverna window that he recalled seeing yesterday. He made a mental note. *Broken nose.*

The scent of her perfume came to him as she approached the spot where he was standing, blocking the walkway. A small frown appeared between her delicate brows even as her lips curved into a lovely smile, bringing a questioning light into her expression.

Her velvet eyes stared into his slate gray ones, and she wondered what messages life had scribbled there to bring such cynicism to the finely molded lips that tightened as he looked down at her from his greater height. She saw emotion that she couldn't define flash like lightning through those stormy depths.

"Hi," he said easily, his glance now open and friendly. All traces of the earlier mood were lost in the warmth of his smile. "Did you enjoy the show last night?"

A glow of happiness highlighted her face as she realized he had noticed her last night and remembered who she was. She schooled herself to remain calm by reminding her impatient heart it was almost twenty-six years old. So he remembered seeing her; so what?

"Why, yes," she replied, pleased at the outer poise she displayed when she really felt breathless and slightly nervous. "Did you?" she asked as he continued to gaze down at her.

"Yes," he said absently. With a startling quickness, he reached out and touched her hair. "Like spun silk," he said, as if to himself. He moved his hand back to his side with obvious reluctance. A frown appeared in his eyes, as if he were displeased with his action.

A tremor ran down Sarah's spine. With devastating insight, she knew why the feelings she'd experienced during her escape had degenerated from the excitement of the first week to the restlessness of the past few days. Because of this man.

She had caught glimpses of him constantly, impressions at the edges of her vision—she hadn't wanted to be caught staring—as he walked past her at the various ancient buildings she had visited. Something about his clean-cut features, his air of purpose, had appealed to her. He had seemed confident, sure of himself and his world: there was an aura of great strength about him. She had known instinctively that he was looking for someone. But not me, she thought, and felt the ridiculous sting of tears for the second time in two days.

"Are you on vacation?" she asked to break the growing silence.

She heard the slight quiver that had invaded her voice. Her life had been so carefully planned and supervised that there had never been an element of mystery in it. Now she sensed a trembling thrill building in her. If he were alone and free . . .

"Yes." His smile quickened across his face. "Getting away from it all," he said in gently mocking tones. "That's the way my secretary put it. She decided I needed a rest, and so here I am." His glance moved all around the area in an encompassing sweep. "I haven't had a vacation in years."

His voice trailed off as he admitted this fact. He seemed reluctant to disclose the information. He probably felt the same way she did, guilty about going but recognizing the need to be free of responsibilities, Sarah thought in instant sympathy. "I understand," she murmured.

He looked at her sympathetic face. "I believe you do," he said solemnly.

She liked his voice, finding it as pleasing to her ears as his clean good looks were to her eyes. The masculine timbre was smoothly modulated, neither bass nor tenor, the cadence manly and controlled. She cleared her throat, trying to think of something to say. He would think her an idiot. But her mind remained painfully devoid of bright chatter. She wondered who he was, where he was from—a thousand personal things.

"If you've finished shopping, how about some lunch?" he invited, nodding toward a nearby outdoor café that catered to the tourist trade. It was a safe open place.

"That would be nice," she said.

At a table under a colorful cabana, he helped her into her chair with a skill that spoke of experience. Well, of course he was used to escorting women, she told herself. A man like him, successful in business, would be successful in social affairs, too. She decided he was in his early thirties. What kind of business was he in? Maybe one of those fast-growing computer companies?

His gray eyes roamed over her in a leisurely appraisal, she noted with pleased surprise as he moved around the table. Did he find her attractive? Or was he just lonesome for a fellow compatriot?

"What kind of business are you getting away from?" she asked.

"Communications systems. The company will design, install, and repair them for you." He sat opposite her, his knees brushing hers. He carefully moved his legs to one side.

Lord help us, he thought, holding a smile on his face with an effort. How am I going to be able to handle this? It was bad enough that the girl and the Brain were one and the same, but worse was the fact that the chief had led him to believe that Sarah Abbot was a shrew, while in reality she was a beautiful little creature, soft-eyed and soft-mouthed. Damn . . . and double damn!

He was filled with self-loathing because he was going

to have to gain her trust through lies, and he was going to have to maintain those lies for the entire trip. The best thing to do was to walk out on this case, but if he did, it might finish his career. Too many refusals wouldn't be tolerated. And the ends justified the means in this business, he added cynically, so why should he be so priggish about his ideals . . .?

"I don't care how you do it," his first supervisor had told him in London years ago. "Just find out what she knows and who told her." His superior had smiled. "She's rich, not bad-looking, and lonely. It shouldn't be hard for you to gain her confidence."

"Doesn't that put us on the same level as the people we're trying to catch?" he had asked.

The smile had faded, and the eyes of the man behind the desk had chilled. "If you think the assignment is too difficult, we can find someone else."

"Good." Mark had stood up and walked out. Using the weaknesses of innocent people to trap others didn't appeal to him. When the sex-and-politics scandal had broken several months later, the lonely divorcée had tried to commit suicide. In Mark's eyes, she had been a harmless victim, someone who'd been guilty only of repeating at a vulnerable moment some indiscreet remarks made to her.

Shortly after that Mark had been assigned to the Paris office, and then to the envoy, where he'd been up until the present. His thoughts returned to Sarah, who watched him with a bright curiosity in her gaze. He couldn't shake the impression that she was a seventeen-year-old innocent.

Actually, from reading her dossier, he'd guessed she was innocent. There had been no long-term boyfriends in her life, and Dr. Fielding should know; the man had monitored every moment of her life from the day her parents had brought her to him.

On her behalf, Mark found himself resenting the intrusions into her privacy. A person ought to have some hidden parts of the soul and mind. Even this escapade wasn't the secret fling that she thought. The psychologist had advised the military brass to let her have this chance to get away on her own. "A classic case of burnout," he had written in his report.

Mark could relate to that. He was feeling the same. He was supposed to be on a real vacation, but this had come up, and the chief had asked him to postpone his leave for another month and find the genius.

Sarah's need for escape had been greater than his, he surmised as he watched the changing expressions cross the delicate contours of her face. Her parents had died in an automobile accident just after Christmas. They had gone to visit her for the holidays and were returning home to North Carolina when the tragedy had occurred. That plus the intense concentration it must have required to break that code had probably brought her to a point of desperation. No wonder she needed to escape.

As he continued to study her he saw wariness creep into her eyes and realized he wasn't playing his part. He forced a smile onto his face. "By the way, I'm Mark Terrington," he said with the correct amount of friendliness.

"Hi. I'm Sarah Abbot," she responded to his expectant look. She had been forced to use her real name because of her passport—because she hadn't known how to get a fake one. No contacts in the underworld, she thought, amused with the idea.

And no chance to make any, part of her mind added. She had been recruited by the military officials and had moved to the vicinity of the Pentagon as soon as she'd completed her advanced degree.

Anguish filled her, shadowing the excitement she felt

at being in this man's company. Because of her move, her bid for freedom, her parents had died. Although they had acknowledged and understood her need to be free from parental dominance, she still felt guilty. And what had she accomplished with her little act of rebellion? Nothing. Not a thing. She had simply exchanged the watchful eyes of her parents and Dr. Fielding for those of the Military Intelligence and the security guards at her apartment building.

She lifted a somber face to the man across from her, and her heart beat a staccato rhythm. Don't, she warned herself. Nothing could come of this chance meeting. This was merely a short vacation, an escape—that was all. Realizing that the silence was again stretching between them, she repeated her first name, thus inviting him to use it. "Sarah. From North Carolina originally." She didn't like to mention Washington, D.C., in connection with herself. People invariably wanted to know if she was in government work.

"Hello, Sarah from North Carolina. I'm Mark from Indiana," he teased. Leaning forward, he took her hand and brought it to his lips in a gesture that seemed completely natural.

The skin on the back of her hand burned where he touched it with his mouth, and she wondered if he could sense the heat she felt inside at the contact. For almost the first time in her life, a man, an *exciting man,* was looking at her as if she were more than some strange specimen in a laboratory. He was looking at her in the way a man peruses a woman that he finds attractive. It was both unnerving and exhilarating.

The waiter came and took their order. Sarah realized that only a few minutes had passed since they'd met, but she felt it had been a lifetime. She felt as though she had known Mark Terrington forever. Her mouth echoed his smile after the waiter left, and to her astonishment, she found herself dropping her head a little so she could look at him through the veil of her lashes. She was flirting as easily as a vamp on a soap opera!

His teasing smile changed, and his gaze left her for a moment to wander in a careless manner over the street nearby. He began to talk about the sights they had seen during the past three days, mentioning that he had noticed her at several of the places. "We must have been following the same tourist guide to the city," he chuckled.

"I used a map given to me by the desk clerk," she murmured.

"Me, too," he said. "It's probably the same one used by all the hotels." He told her where he was staying and that it was just down the street from her hotel.

He couldn't stop himself from watching as she lifted the first bite of food to her mouth when the lunch was served. She had the most alluring mouth. Her lips looked incredibly soft. He could imagine them under his, responding with a passion that would match his own desire.

A breeze ruffled the curls that covered her head. He wanted to touch them again. He wanted to touch her all over. A surging pain in his body warned him away from those thoughts.

Sarah worried about the sudden silences between them. They would talk, exploring politely into each other's lives, then lapse into unspoken thoughts, both of them introspective. He was probably wishing he were a thousand miles from her. Why couldn't she think of something to say?

Mark found himself slipping into the role of pursuer easily . . . too easily. Again and again his thoughts roamed away from the mundane topics they were conversing about. He wondered how she would feel in his arms. Small and soft, came the answer from deep inside him. The aching desire returned, sweeping upward into his chest until the pressure threatened to choke him.

He watched her eat, the movements of her mouth enticing him to sample her lips himself. When she twisted in her chair to glance down the street while she told him of some item she had seen in a store down that way, he nearly groaned aloud. The movement caused her breasts to thrust against her knitted top, and the seam line of her bra was vaguely discernible through the cloth. It was the sexiest thing he had ever seen.

What would her nipples look like? Small and pert, as the rest of her was? Or larger, plumper, surprising him with their delicate fullness?

Her skin would be smooth. He would trace the lines of her bathing suit, the demarcation between the tanned and the white skin, until she writhed with the ecstasy of his touch, until she begged him with her velvety eyes to take her, until her voice grew husky murmuring his name.

He would touch her and stroke her and explore all of her. . . .

"Well, I guess we should go," Sarah said uncertainly. They had long since finished their meal, and she had run out of words again. She stood when he did.

He walked her back to her hotel. On the way, for no logical reason, he suddenly felt an overwhelming sense of danger. Glancing at the small lovely woman who walked beside him, he knew the cause. He was already becoming involved with her. He decided to tell the chief to get someone else for the job, but when they stopped in the hotel lobby, he heard himself asking her for a date that night.

Once in her room, Sarah fell onto the neatly made

bed. She called herself all kinds of names. Then she pressed her face into a pillow and hid a silly, happy smile that she couldn't suppress.

Mark. Mark Terrington. From Indiana. Tycoon of communications equipment. With dark hair that had an unruly curl to it as it blew over his forehead, tossed by the May breeze. Her fingers itched to smooth it back, to ruffle through the dark shining strands.

Delicately her hand touched the fluff of curls over her ear. He had touched her there. He had said her hair was like spun silk—before he had retreated behind that friendly but opaque facade. She would like him to touch her again.

Mark Terrington. With eyes as impenetrable as slate . . . except for the few moments during their luncheon when they'd been unguarded. What had he been thinking then?

Mark. His face wasn't truly handsome but was clean-cut, with neat planes and slight depressions under his cheekbones that gave him a lean, hard appearance. He was smooth-shaven, with a firm chin and wonderful mouth.

She rubbed the back of her hand where he had kissed it. Why had he done that?

There had been an alert intelligence in his eyes, and his conversation, though not profound, had indicated refinement and education. Or was she imagining traits she hoped were present?

Her face became serious. Don't, she warned her heart. Don't read more into his sexy looks and friendly manner than had been there. Don't expect anything great to come of this. Don't wish. Don't dream. Don't yearn.

"Don't breathe," she muttered with an ache in her chest.

She napped, waking with an exclamation to check

the clock. Time to take a bath and get ready for their date. As she gathered clean clothes and laid them on the bed, she thought about how little time they'd have together. In a few days, her trip on the freighter would start, and she would have to leave Mark behind.

A brilliant idea came to her. Maybe Mark could come on the cruise, too. He had said he had no set plans, was free to do as he wished. Perhaps she would mention it later that night.

She was tense during their dinner at one of Athens' most expensive restaurants, and even more so when Mark asked her to dance. The husky tone of his voice and his sexy smile made her wonder at his mood.

The dress she wore was the most fetching she had ever owned. The white fitted bodice was shot with silver threads, and the black skirt swished around her knees with a delightfully silky feel. The low neckline dropped deeply between her breasts. Mark's gratifying surprise when he'd seen her step off the elevator earlier that evening had brought a blush of pleasure to her face that had stayed.

As they danced he folded her deeper into his embrace until he held her tightly against his chest. His fingers caressed her waist. "You smell good," he murmured against her hair.

"Thank you," she whispered.

He became somewhat withdrawn after that, and she couldn't find an opportunity to bring up her trip. When he walked her to the door of her hotel room, she was washed by a wave of desperation.

"Will you go sight-seeing with me tomorrow and the next day and the next?" he asked.

"Yes," she answered. "Oh, but I leave on my cruise Friday. So we only have Wednesday and Thursday." She took her courage in both hands. "Since you don't have any plans and . . . and if there's room on the freighter, I thought it might be fun for you to come on the voyage. That is, if you like that sort of thing." Abruptly she stopped speaking and looked up at him.

"Thank you, Sarah," he said solemnly. "I would like that very much." Bending, he brushed his lips very lightly across hers. Then he left.

2

~~**⊶∽∞∞∞∞∞∞∞∞∽⊷**~~

I can't believe you're here," Sarah exclaimed to Mark, standing next to him on the deck of the freighter. "Yesterday when you told me there had been a last-minute cancellation, I was sure you had misunderstood or had the wrong ship or something like that." She laughed up at him, excitement brightening her brown eyes.

He grinned at her, but she sensed a restraint in him and turned back to watch the activity on the wharf rather than let him see the hesitant frown developing on her brow. She wondered what he was thinking that seemed to take him so far from her side. This wasn't the first time during the past few days that she had sensed his withdrawal from her.

An elderly couple were coming up the ramp, and one of the deckhands went down to help them, taking charge of the luggage and directing them to their cabin in guttural tones. He evidently didn't speak much

English. In fact, no one on the boat did. That had surprised her.

Mark monitored the activity below with a practiced surveillance. He was intensely aware of the woman at his side. He was angry with himself for the lies he had told her and, perversely, with her for falling into his hands so easily. When she had suggested he come on the trip, that had solved all his problems about finagling his way into the position of being her escort.

As if she were aware of his train of thought, she suddenly asked, "What do you think happened to the other passenger, the one who canceled?"

He decided to tell her the truth. "He got a chance to exchange his ticket for one on a luxury liner along with a hefty amount of cash for spending money."

She wasn't slow about catching on. "Oh, but you shouldn't have wasted your money like that!"

The slate gray eyes looked into hers. "I didn't consider it a waste."

He watched the pleased flush spread over her face and felt his stomach muscles tighten. Dammit, his job was to let her have her fling, not to seduce her. He and his partner, Kelly Achinson—who was playing the role of Baruch the deckhand—were to watch over her and protect her at all costs.

At all costs, he mused soberly. Yes, there was no question that he would do that. "What?" He spoke guiltily, realizing she had asked him something. He had to stop going off into these trances, thinking about her.

"Where did the captain go?"

"I think I saw him up on the bridge earlier."

"When do you think we will get under way?"

He shrugged his broad shoulders. "Probably not for another couple of hours. Anxious to be off on your adventure?" he teased.

Her mouth curved upward into an enchanting line

that faltered slightly when he quickly looked away. She knew he was thinking of much more than his expression showed. She noticed the way his gaze roamed over the pier. She, too, glanced around. She had the feeling he was looking for someone. Perhaps he had fallen in love with the wife of some rich man whose yacht was here at Piraiévs, and he hoped to see her before the freighter left on its odyssey around the islands. And perhaps, just perhaps, she should never have come on this trip.

She thought of her friend, Jennifer, who had gotten the information about the cargo ship and made the reservations for her. Jennifer's husband was in the army, and his best friend had married a Greek girl, whose father was Captain Theodopoulos, owner of the vessel. A pensive sadness flickered through her.

"What are you thinking?"

The smooth voice brought her back to the present. Mark's eyes were gentle as he looked at her. "About a friend. She had a miscarriage a few months ago. It's very hard for her to conceive, and she's afraid she might not be able to again."

Her simple statement hung on the air between them, establishing a rapport. Sarah felt as though Mark understood her inner anguish, the tears she had held back as she comforted her friend.

People needed people, she realized. Did this strong man ever need anyone? Did he ever crave the soft comfort of a woman's arms? She would like to be the one he turned to.

His hand lifted to her face, and he brushed at the corner of her eye. "My grandmother once told me there was no gift greater than a gentle-hearted woman," he said in husky tones.

She shook her head and stepped back against the railing, away from his burning touch. "I'm not," she denied.

"Aren't you?" he questioned softly. It was his turn to look thoughtful. "Not many people, male or female, are." He nodded toward the cabins. "Let's unpack before the ship gets going. We'll want to watch the scenery once we depart. Dinner will be late tonight, Baruch said." He checked over the crowds on the shore once more before he moved off toward his cabin, which was down the companionway from Sarah's.

He would be sleeping just on the other side of the wall from her, she realized. A premonition raced along her nerves. She didn't know what the strange sensation meant, but she realized that she was about to embark on her own voyage of discovery. Would she, like Jason, find a treasure of Golden Fleece?

Or maybe she would get fleeced, she reminded herself wryly. Briefly, she wondered about the elderly couple who had smiled and nodded and gone on to their cabin. She thought they had been speaking German. Who else was on this ship? The captain, of course, and two deckhands. And the freighter would have a cook, maybe a cook's helper.

Taking out the few dresses she had brought, she hung them in the small closet, then put her slacks and tops in a chest, her other items in the tiny bath. Her mind continued to roam, and all her thoughts flew like homing pigeons to the one man who had ever totally captivated her attention and imagination. Was it only the magic of being on this forbidden holiday that made him seem so fascinating? Or was it more than that?

Just as she finished storing the last articles, the engine started and they began to move. She rushed out on deck. Mark was at the railing. Her heart beat fast, and she spoke almost shyly. "We're leaving now?"

"Yes." His eyes swept over her in a manner that brought a surge of warm blood to her face. "Are you ready for your Greek adventure to begin?"

She nodded, afraid to speak. She was trembling with excitement. A strange, primitive urgency had invaded her insides.

"Our steward said we were going to make a side trip to one of the smaller islands to pick up a load of pistachios before we go on down to Sounion."

"I see," she murmured, watching as the wharf receded and the freighter slowly backed out into the channel.

The elderly couple came through the companionway to the starboard side. Mark spoke to them and the three conversed for several minutes, then he introduced Sarah.

"Sarah, Mr. and Mrs. Jeddermann from Munich. They are traveling for her health. She is worried about being seasick."

"I have some medicine," Sarah quickly offered, but they had something of their own, Mr. Jeddermann assured her, using Mark as an interpreter.

Baruch came up to them. "Passports, please," he said in a thick accent. He followed the couple back to their cabin.

Mark left Sarah at her door and moved away with the easy swinging stride that was indicative of his confidence and poise. He wasn't an ordinary tourist, she thought as she got her passport and returned to the deck. He wasn't an ordinary *anything*, she laughed to herself.

"Give me your passport," his voice said behind her, startling her. She hadn't heard his approach. He had a totally silent walk. "I'll take it to Baruch. I know you don't want to miss any of the sights."

"Thanks." She handed over the document.

He opened it and studied her photograph, which didn't do her justice at all. He looked at her. "Your hair, it's different."

Her small hand fingered the fluff of curls. "I had it cut and frizzed the day I left the States."

"I like it." His hand touched where hers had been only a second before, his fingers smoothing the curly softness away from her temple. "Soft," he said and abruptly spun around and strode away.

She stood frozen where he'd left her, feeling an incredible rush of warmth through her veins. She knew with some primitive female instinct that he liked her. That wonderfully strong, virile male liked her . . . for herself. But would he if he knew what she really was?

On the trip from Aegina, the tiny island where they picked up the nuts, to Sounion, Sarah stayed glued to the railing, not wanting to miss one glimpse of the magnificent coastline, with its white beaches and towering cliffs. Toward evening, they put in at the port of Sounion, a few miles south of Athens.

She had met the captain and the rest of the crew, which consisted of a mate, an engineer, a cook, and the two deckhands, Baruch and Giorgio. She, Mark, and the Jeddermanns occupied the three passenger cabins. Feeling that her life had only now begun, Sarah turned to Mark.

He leaned on the railing, his arms and shoulders well developed and powerful. He had left his shirt partially open, and she liked the fact that the hair on his chest wasn't awfully thick, only a neat patch across his breastbone. His skin was evenly tanned.

Following his glance down to the dock, she saw Captain Theodopoulos come out of a building with another man; a local merchant, she assumed. They looked over the wares the captain had brought out, a collection of small pottery vases. She realized the seaman must trade in tourist items, probably supplying the islands from the factories on the mainland.

"I wish I could understand what they were saying. How did you learn Greek?" She looked back at Mark.

"Business contacts and the army. I was stationed here."

"And you spoke to the Jeddermanns in German. Do you speak other languages?" she asked, openly prying.

"The so-called Romance languages; a smattering of Arabic." He shrugged as if the accomplishment were nothing.

She looked displeased with herself. "I've never been good at things like that. Languages aren't logical," she complained, then clamped her teeth together in chagrin.

"What do you mean?" He shot her a glance from gray eyes, catching her hesitation as she nibbled on her lower lip.

Don't be so smart, she cautioned. Men are not impressed with brains in a woman. "Well, if the plural of mouse is mice, why isn't the plural of house, hice?" She slanted him a smiling challenge, pleased with her silly answer.

He laughed aloud, and she loved the sound, so warm and rippling in the deepening evening light. They lapsed into silence as the last brilliant flare of the setting sun turned the ruins of the Temple of Poseidon into a dazzling pink and gold sculpture. His hand touched, then clasped hers in a spirit of togetherness that was new to her.

For the first time in her life, Sarah felt totally alive. All her senses were awake. For once, she was a creature of sensation and intuition instead of logic. Her earlier premonition returned. She knew she wouldn't finish this trip as she had started it, in a gay mood of defiance, but she would be changed in a way that would mark her for life. Marked by Mark Terrington.

Her misgivings slowly disappeared, giving way to another notion. She *wanted* to be touched by him. Don't, she warned her heart, don't get your hopes built to the sky on pipe dreams. He was a wonderful person who seemed genuinely interested in her. That did not mean he was going to fall head over heels in love with her! she reminded herself with painful honesty.

He released her hand and walked away, going toward his cabin without a word. She was glad that he didn't look back, for her face was suffused with yearning—yearning for him to stay.

She had her emotions under control when Mark knocked at her door and escorted her to dinner. The dining salon was a tiny room below deck, located next to an even tinier galley. The cook was also the waiter. He conveyed the captain's apologies for not joining them.

"The Jeddermanns won't be coming down, either," Mark said, interpreting the information for Sarah. "The wife has taken to her bed, and they are having dinner in their room. I don't think the voyage is going to be much fun for them."

His expression was once again abstracted. Sarah worried that the voyage might not be much fun for him. She had suggested that he come. Was she supposed to entertain him? But as they ate, a quiet sense of contentment grew between them, and she relaxed completely in his company.

The mood was broken by the entry of Baruch. The swarthy sailor said something to Mark after nodding to her. The man had a forbidding quality about him in spite of his smile, and Sarah found herself recoiling from his presence. He went into the galley, then returned a minute later with a cup of coffee. He paused by the table, his dark eyes going to Mark. For a second, Sarah thought there was tension between the two men, then Baruch walked out.

"Shall we go up?" Mark asked later, after the cook had served dessert. They met Giorgio coming down the companionway with a tray of half-eaten food. He smiled broadly at the young couple, then spoke to Mark.

"The other passengers aren't faring well," Mark explained.

Sarah felt sorry for the seasick traveler. "It's nice of her husband to stay with her," she said.

He gave her a cryptic look. "Wouldn't you expect him to?"

He walked to the railing without waiting for an answer, and they watched the activity onshore. Night had fallen, and the tavernas were bright with lights and laughter.

"Sailors come and go," she mused, a touch of envy on her face. "Always free, as free as the four winds and the seven seas." She sighed.

"Freedom can be lonely," Mark said softly. "A life on the sea may sound romantic, but it's dull, hard work, most often. And a roaming man has few friends and no home."

Sarah considered his statements. Was he lonely? Surely he had tons of friends. Or were they only business contacts, like most of the people she knew?

He abruptly changed the subject. "Would you like to go ashore? There's a good club for bouzouki, if you're interested."

"Sounds great. Is this okay to wear?" She indicated her casual clothing of slacks and blouse.

"Perfect," he said, making a survey of her curves.

She hurried to her cabin to freshen up, thrilled at the prospect of going out with someone like him. Someone like him? What did she know about Mark Terrington? That he was handsome, friendly, sexy . . . and everytime he looked at her, the bottom fell out of her heart!

Cool it, she told herself firmly, going back on deck and leaning on the railing as she waited for him. A couple strolled along the harbor. She recognized them and impulsively waved.

They waved back, then moved on. A stirring of air alerted her to Mark's presence, and she turned to him with a smile.

The nightspot was close by. When they were seated at a small table, Mark ordered wine for them. *"Aresinato,"* he told the waiter, then turned to her. "That's the kind without the resin."

She was relieved. Shielding her mouth with her hand, she whispered to him, "Wine that tastes like turpentine smells is not my cup of tea, if you'll excuse the metaphor."

"I know what you mean," he replied gravely, his eyes gleaming in the candlelight.

The Grecian music wove a magic cloth about them. At first it was haunting and simple, but as the night wore on—the Greeks didn't seem to get started until after ten in the evening—the rhythms became faster.

"Let's try it," Mark invited, holding out a hand to her.

Some of the people had their arms about one another's shoulders as they danced in an undulating line. Clasping her securely with his long fingers, Mark joined them onto one end of it. Her other hand was taken by a stranger, a young man who smiled encouragingly at her dismayed countenance.

"Mark, I don't know how to do this!"

"You'll catch on."

They started moving, first in one direction, then the other. The movements were similar to the dances she had seen in Athens during the past few days. Soon her nimble mind was anticipating the steps and her feet followed naturally. They danced faster. Faster. She was breathless with enjoyment when they finished to a loud shout. "Hai!" she shouted with the crowd.

She was aware of her handsome escort and the glow of approval in his eyes as they tried another fast-paced dance, then another. At one point in the evening, plates were thrown, smashing into fragments that were crushed into smaller bits by stamping feet.

"Watch your eyes," Mark warned, raising a hand to protect her face from flying pieces.

Two men danced over the shards, lithe and agile in their youth and strength. The audience began to clap in time as the tempo increased. The music grew louder, more demanding.

Like making love, she thought, glancing over to find Mark's eyes roaming over her with a possessive light. Her heart beat in time to the wildly tempestuous music; her hands clapped harder until they hurt.

It was two o'clock in the morning when they left.

"Excuse me, do you speak English?" A man with a British accent stopped them at the door.

The arm around her waist tensed to rock hardness, and Mark's fingers closed tightly over her hip, bringing her against his side as if they were lovers. His touch made her feel secure.

"Yes," Mark answered.

"I was wondering if you could tell me how I can get into Athens in the morning? I need to go as early as possible," he requested.

"You could try the bus; number 50, I think, goes into the city. It leaves from the harbor stop before seven."

"Before seven? Delightful. Thank you very much." He raised a hand in a gesture of farewell and strode off.

Sarah was surprised to see a muscle knot in Mark's

jaw as if he were gritting his teeth. He snapped out of his absorption as they were jostled by people who were now in a hurry to get home and get some sleep before another workday started.

"Let's go," he said quietly.

At the freighter, she stopped in front of her door. "Thank you for a lovely evening," she murmured. It wasn't until he reached around her and opened the door that she realized she was waiting for his good-night kiss. Quickly she stepped inside with another awkwardly mumbled good night and thanks.

"Good night, Sarah," he said, her name coming from his lips as if he said it often. He closed the door after her. "Lock it," he ordered.

She turned the button and heard him check to make sure it was secure before he left. Going to the tiny built-in bureau, she pulled out nylon pajamas and put them on. The bottoms had long legs, while the top had an elastic neckline with a lace ruffle. In the bathroom, she washed her face and brushed her teeth, trying to be sparing with the water. The captain probably had to buy it at the ports they visited.

She turned out the light and lay on her bed without pulling down the top sheet. The music of the taverna hummed through her restless mind. She was very tired from the long, busy day, and yet her body refused to relax.

Her thoughts wandered over the events of the evening and settled on the tension she had sensed between Mark and Baruch. Had she only imagined that moment down in the dining salon? And why the jaw-clenching tautness when the Englishman had approached them about transportation to Athens? His drawing her to his side had been an instinctive, protective reaction. If there had been trouble, Mark would have pushed her behind him. She was positive of that. But why had he reacted with such quick reflexes? It was as if he had been trained to do that.

But, she reasoned, he was a protective person, and he had been in the army. He was wealthy and traveling alone. Naturally he would be wary. She, too, had better be more on guard. She knew she tended to be too trusting. Not that anyone knew who she was, but still she should be cautious, she decided. With her line of work and all . . . and being on her own.

She had Mark. His actions had already indicated that he would take care of her. Or had she completely misread the situation?

The flare of a lighter outside her window brought her upright. Silently she crawled out of bed and went across to the porthole.

A powerful masculine figure stood on the deck, one hip braced against the railing. A red glow moved from the vicinity of his thigh to his mouth and back again. He held his cigarette in his left hand, she surmised. It was the second time she had seen him smoke. Apparently he didn't have the vice as a regular habit. On an impulse that she didn't try to suppress, she slipped on her robe and went outside barefoot.

He tossed the cigarette overboard. It made a glowing arc across the water before landing with a quick hiss and disappearing. "What are you doing out here?" His tone was gruff, as if he were displeased by her appearance.

"I couldn't sleep. I . . . I was too wound up," she explained. "The music and everything."

That sounded like the lamest excuse in the world, she thought. He would laugh at her. Feeling more foolish than she ever had, she turned to go back to her room.

"Whoa, don't run off as soon as you get here," he said on a note of amusement. He reached out a hand and pulled her to the railing beside him. "I kept you up too late."

As if he were talking to a child, she fumed. She wanted him to see her as a woman, mature and sophisticated. "I don't want to disturb you," she said stiffly.

That was greeted with a choked laugh. "Don't you?" His question had a double meaning.

"No," she said quietly, with dignity. Never again would she give in to impulse. She was too logical for this type of behavior, acting like a starry-eyed girl instead of a twenty-five-year-old woman. She moved in his grasp, wanting to escape.

"Stay," he requested, and she did.

The sense of danger was strong in Mark, as strong as it had been in Athens. The scar on his left arm throbbed. He knew now that the threat was real, from outside, although undefined as yet. He would know more when he met with the British agent in the morning.

He was relieved that it wasn't only his attraction for Sarah that had brought forth the feeling of danger. His instincts were still in good working order, but his worries for her were now increased tenfold. It was hard enough to protect a person with her knowledge of military secrets: it was much harder to do it and keep her in the dark, too.

Sarah shivered slightly, and his arm came around her shoulders, hugging her to his warm chest. For a moment, she resisted his touch; then she relaxed against him, turning in to him a little more, letting her arms slide naturally around his lean waist.

Heat radiated through the layers of material to warm her breasts with his masculine fire. She sighed, a sound of contentment and excitement. "You make me feel funny," she whispered.

He shifted his leg on the railing, cradling her more deeply into the sheltering cove of his thighs. His hand lifted and began to stroke sensuously through her soft curls. "Sarah," he murmured.

Was that a note of despair in his ragged utterance? It was as if he were asking her to spare him some grief—grief that she herself might bring him. Her arms tightened, offering an unspoken and unasked for comfort.

His finger drew a semicircle around her ear and followed her cheek to her mouth. There he tortured the tender flesh that yearned for his mouth with lingering caresses along her bottom lip.

"Your mouth is so soft." His voice was hoarse. "Nice and soft. So very nice."

She tried not to let her lips tremble as he awakened passion throughout her being with his searching finger. He probed deeper. He roamed over her teeth with a natural curiosity, as if testing the texture of their surface. He discovered a minuscule rough edge along one lower tooth and explored this, rubbing back and forth slowly.

When he withdrew from inside her lips, he continued to play with his moist fingertip along the corner of her mouth, eliciting a strange sensation that made her gasp.

She reached up and caught his wrist, bringing his hand away from her tormented mouth. "Don't."

His chest moved in silent laughter, and he slid closer to her along the railing. "Why?" he mocked her lightly.

Her fingertips recorded the ridge along his inner arm. "How did you get this scar?" She asked a question of her own.

"A knife slipped," was his laconic reply.

"Not yours," she said immediately, "or if it was, you weren't the one holding it."

The awareness between them changed. "Why do you say that?" he asked after a beat of time.

"It's the wrong direction. The slant is wrong." She traced it with her fingers. "The point went in here, slashed down this way. You had your left arm up, defending yourself."

"Brilliant conclusion," he complimented her.

"What happened?"

Her worry was sincere, and it showed in her voice as she persisted with the interrogation. She sensed his withdrawal before he even shifted his position so that he could stand and move away from her.

Against the night sky, his shoulders moved in a shrug. "I was in the army. What would you expect of a soldier?" he demanded coldly. "It was the usual brawl."

She absorbed this. "Did he live?" she asked soberly.

"Yes, he got away before I could kill him," he answered brutally, deliberately making her wince.

There was a long silence between them. All that had passed before, during their days in Athens and the evening here at Sounion, was destroyed in the shocking statement and resulting hush. Sarah realized that the strength she had admired in Mark Terrington could also be a granite hardness that was unyielding.

"You're different," she said.

Both of his hands gripped the metal of the railing, and his arms were stiff as he leaned on them. "From what?" he asked cynically. "From what you thought? Are you disappointed?"

He had seen so much more of the world than she had. She couldn't begin to fathom the experiences he had lived through. They had etched a bitterness into his soul like an acid burn. But there would be healing. Whatever had happened to him would fade. The scars might not be pretty, but they would cover the wounds.

"Mark . . ."

"You'd better go in, Sarah," he said firmly. "We leave tomorrow, and I have to . . . make a couple of calls before we do."

"You'll hardly have had any sleep." She worried

about his lack of rest and the fact that he seemed to be working during his vacation. Why the sudden need to work?

He crossed the decking and opened the door that led to the cabins, impatient for her to be gone. "It doesn't matter. I've survived on less."

She went docilely into her cabin once more, anger flaring in a quick spurt at his ungracious manner as he closed the door behind her.

"Lock it," he ordered as he had earlier, waiting until she did before he walked off.

Flinging off her robe, she flopped onto the hard mattress, kicking aside the covering sheet. She didn't know why she was so upset, except that one minute he had been sweet and gentle, the next almost like a lover, and finally, impatient and hasty with her. She was almost positive he was attracted to her, but each time she thought he was going to deepen their friendship, he withdrew.

Steps sounded on the ramp outside, and she listened intently to find out if Mark was leaving. He probably had a girl in town that he was meeting on the sly.

"I just got back," a man said, sounding breathless. She recognized the voice of the sailor, Baruch. "Have you . . .?"

"Sarah," Mark interrupted, but that was all she understood, because he spoke the remainder of his sentence in Greek. Their voices faded as they moved off down the deck, talking in low tones.

A relieved smile appeared on her face as she realized that Mark wasn't going ashore after all. Not that she had any right whatsoever to censor his movements, but the thought of him going to meet another woman was unbearable. In a few short days, her feelings for him had gone far beyond a casual attraction.

They were strangers and yet, impossible as it seemed,

she felt that they had always known each other. Intuitively she recognized him. It had nothing to do with logic.

Dr. Fielding would probably have her locked up if he could see into her mind at this moment, she chuckled to herself. The delicate lips pressed together defiantly. What the dear doctor didn't know needn't concern him.

Her eyelashes sank upon the curve of her cheek, and she yawned sleepily. She wished she and Mark were alone on a world cruise and that they would never have to see anyone else ever again, especially the grouchy deckhand, Baruch. She wondered what he and Mark were talking about. Her eyes snapped open.

The man had spoken perfect English to Mark when he came aboard!

3

Smuggling: That was the first niggling thought in Sarah's mind when she woke up a few hours later. Glancing out the porthole, she saw the sun was up, and she, too, rose, going into the small bathroom and taking a quick shower to refresh her tired body. During her restless sleep, she had fretted constantly about Baruch and his pretense at not speaking English.

Why did it bother her so much? Because of Mark, she admitted. What had he and the deckhand talked about in the wee hours of the morning? Had Mark been waiting for Baruch to return to the ship? Was that why he had been so impatient with her arrival on the deck? Had they planned some smuggling operation?

Remembering the feel of Mark's arms around her, she found herself denying that he could be mixed up in something illegal. Her logical mind and her illogical heart wrangled over the problem.

Well, she decided grumpily, she would keep her eyes and ears open and see what happened. What could she do, anyway? Try to make Mark see the error of his ways? Then what? A knock on her door brought dark pensive eyes up to stare at it apprehensively. Shaking off a feeling of doom, she called out "Yes" in a steady voice.

"Breakfast is ready." It was Mark who answered. "There's a place on deck where we can eat if you'd like."

"That would be nice. I'll be out in a sec." She found her bathing suit, slipped it on, and pulled a gauze caftan over it. A fluff of her hair with a wide-toothed comb and she was ready. She unlocked and opened the door.

The smile on her face was forced only until she saw Mark's appreciative countenance; then it became real, reflecting off his own smile like the sun off the dancing waves of the sea. The doubts of the early morning darkness receded, then disappeared like a fog.

"Good morning," he said in a deeply vibrant voice.

He simply couldn't be dishonest, she mused, returning his greeting and following him until they reached a table near the bow of the freighter. She noticed that a canvas had been laced through overhead supports to give shade to that part of the deck. Then all her attention focused on Mark as they sat down.

He would be very easy to fall in love with was her next brilliant thought. Silently she ate the meal of fresh croissants, eggs, and fruit, letting him carry most of the conversation. After that, he seemed content to sit near her, relaxing.

Giorgio came to take the trays. He reported that the other couple had been to the dining salon for breakfast, but that Mrs. Jeddermann had felt worse later and had returned to her cabin. They were all invited to have dinner with the captain that night.

Mark went to his room to get some reports, which he

then proceeded to read in the shade of the awning. Sarah removed her caftan and stretched out on a bench in the sun. Closing her eyes, she was asleep in a few minutes. Later she woke briefly as she was lifted in careful arms and deposited on a covered pad in the shade.

"Thank you," she said drowsily.

"My pleasure," he murmured. His lips skimmed her temple as he put her down. He stood there a minute after she settled back into slumber. It wasn't going to be easy to deceive her. He doubted that they could do it for the entire cruise. Shaking his head, he went back to his reports, which were interesting articles on the latest in communications equipment.

Sarah woke to a nudge on her shoulder. "Where are we?" she wanted to know, rising and stretching luxuriously.

"Just past Hydra," Mark said. "How about some exercise?"

Prodding her along, he insisted on walking briskly around the deck for a full half hour before he let her rest again. After lunch, he went to his cabin, and she didn't see him for the rest of the afternoon. Restless, she explored all around the freighter, even taking a quick peek into the storage holds. She watched the crew at their tasks and waved to the captain as she passed the bridge. She spoke to Mr. Jeddermann and tried to ask about his wife without success.

Sitting on the guardrail, she lifted her gaze upward to the cliffs and rugged terrain as they came into Nauplia, a state capital and thriving seaport on the Gulf of Argolis. This city showed the influence of several cultures: Turkish, Venetian, and Greek.

She had taken a five-day bus trip through this region during her first week in Greece. It would be worth seeing again. Epidaurus wasn't far, nor Mycenae, where Agamemnon had been king. Corinth was only about twenty-five miles north.

"How long will we be here? Do you know?" she asked Mark when he joined her.

"All day tomorrow, according to the schedule," he said. "We'll be leaving early Monday morning for Mykonos."

A whole day, she mused. Sunday was a lovely day for lazy sight-seeing. Maybe Mark would invite her to go with him. She waited, but he said nothing further.

As evening lingered over the gulf, providing a backdrop for the mountainous land, she was seized with a multitude of emotions induced by the slow fading of the enchanted day, the rugged beauty of the land, and the memory, somehow primal, of the grandeur it had once known. Coupled with this was the preknowledge of the despair she would know when the trip was over. One vacation, eternally remembered. That had to be better than having *nothing* to remember.

She glanced up to find Mark studying the fleeting expressions that raced across her face, and she thought she saw pity in his eyes. She looked away.

An hour later she was called from her room by a knock on her door. She went down to dinner. Both the Jeddermanns were present, and the captain proved to be a charming, talkative host. With Mark interpreting for all of them, the conversation moved along, although slowly due to the repetitions, and they chatted of past vacations until quite late. When the dinner broke up, Mark returned to his cabin, saying nothing to Sarah.

Feeling lonely, she went in to her cabin and took off her dress, then slipped into clean slacks and a long-sleeved shirt. She went to the starboard deck.

Going over to the shaded spot, she sat in a lounge chair and watched the lights onshore. There were the usual tourists milling around, soaking up the local color. Next month and throughout the summer, there would be many more visitors to this area, who would come to see the plays still put on each June and July at the amphitheater at Epidaurus.

A whiff of cologne and tobacco warned her that Mark was near, although she never heard his silent footfalls. Instead of seeking her out as she expected, he turned and went down the gangplank to shore. He, too, had changed clothes, and was now wearing dark slacks and a dark shirt that almost made him invisible.

She noticed the breadth of his shoulders and the strength of his arms as he walked along the waterfront. She wondered where he could be going at this hour. She was still wondering when she went to bed at midnight.

Baruch served her breakfast the next morning. She was the only one in the dining salon.

"Kali Mera," she said, determined that he was going to speak to her.

"Kali Mera," he muttered. He went into the galley.

A few minutes later she called out her thanks after choking down a roll and a cup of coffee. She went topside.

The day was extraordinarily lovely, but she was filled with misery. She wasn't able to fool herself: Mark hadn't come in last night. Did he have a woman in port here?

Baruch appeared on deck. He pointed toward the wharf where a man approached. Sarah assumed that the two had business about some cargo. She nodded, and he went ashore. Giorgio and the captain came out of a warehouse adjacent to the dock, and all four men stood together, talking with a great deal of enthusiasm, presumably about the freight business.

Sarah wondered about Baruch's antagonistic attitude toward her and his refusal to speak English when she knew perfectly well that he could. As the men disappeared into the warehouse, she briefly considered the possibility that the whole crew was involved in a smuggling operation. Then she berated herself for the thought. The only person acting in the least suspicious was Mark.

She went to his door and knocked in case he had returned while she was below. "Mark?" she called softly. No answer; no sound of any kind in his room. She turned and went down the ramp to shore, deciding to go for a walk.

Spotting a restaurant, she went in and ordered fresh croissants and hot tea along with butter and a pot of honey. She ate with a kind of defiant relish. Finished, she licked her fingers and settled back with a last cup of tea. What could she do today?

A couple came into the place and stood at the door, looking around while their eyes adjusted from the bright sunshine to the dim interior. When the girl's eyes met Sarah's, they widened in recognition. A smile spread over her face.

With an impulsive gesture, Sarah indicated that they were welcome to join her. Immediately she thought better of it. They were on their honeymoon, she recalled, and wouldn't want company.

But the young blonde woman tugged at the man's arm and, noticing Sarah, he came across the room with his wife.

"Good morning," he said with a heavy accent. His hair was a medium brown, but his eyes were as blue as his wife's. The couple was the epitome of healthy good looks. "May we join you?"

Sarah smiled brightly. "Yes, please do. I remember seeing you in Athens. You checked into the hotel where

I was staying," she reminded him since he didn't seem to remember her.

"Ah, yes," he said, his memory still apparently unstirred.

"And we saw you on the deck of a ship at Sounion. We waved, but we did not know if you recognized us," his wife added. Her accent wasn't quite as pronounced.

Swedish, Sarah thought. "Where are you from?" she inquired after they had sat down.

"Austria," the woman answered. "I am Anna, and this is my husband, Will Arnheim."

He bowed solemnly from the waist. "How do you do?"

Sarah returned the greeting, pleased with their intriguing blend of friendliness and formality. Anna was the more outgoing of the two.

The couple ordered a light breakfast, and the three of them talked while it was prepared. The discussion of sights they had visited continued during the meal and afterward, over fresh cups of tea.

"I loved Epidaurus," Sarah exclaimed. "The theater was part of a medical complex, you know. Those ruins are there, too. Be sure to explore all of them."

Anna raised a beaming face to Sarah. "Why do you not join us in going there?" she invited.

"Well," Sarah began, not sure that she should.

"We have our own car. We can come back when we want, if you have other engagements," Anna continued.

Sarah quickly thought it over. She had no commitments for the day; therefore, there was no reason for not going with them. But she had better check in at the freighter in case Mark had returned. If he hadn't, she could tell Baruch her plans.

"I'll just run back and leave a message," she decided, jumping to her feet.

Only Giorgio was on the freighter when she climbed aboard. She spared a thought for the elderly couple. Where were they? There was no sign that Mark had ever returned. The soft lips compressed.

"I'm going sight-seeing," she told Giorgio. He smiled widely, obviously not understanding. "Epidaurus," she elaborated. He smiled and nodded. Giving up, she went to her room.

Checking her purse for Greek money, she wondered uneasily about her passport, which was locked in the ship's safe. But she wasn't leaving the country, so there was no reason to carry it. She jotted down her itinerary and stuck it on her door with a Band-Aid, and left the ship again. Anna and Will were further along the street when she returned. She hurried to them, apologizing for keeping them waiting.

"That is all right," Anna said. "All is okay?"

Sarah grinned at the use of the universal slang term. "All is okay," she agreed cheerily. If she wasn't quite as happy as she sounded, there was no reason for them to know it. She stepped briskly along to the rental car parked at the curb.

They climbed in, the couple in front and Sarah in back, and Will started the engine. Carefully he maneuvered along the hilly terrain until he could pick up speed on the winding mountain road.

Sarah watched the scenery passing by and chatted with Anna. They tried to identify the trees: pines, locust, cypress, a grove of olives. All along, though, she couldn't help wondering where Mark was and what he was doing.

They reached the ruins before noon, and visited the sanctuary of Aesculapius, the god of healing and therapy. The temple was large, about forty by eighty feet.

A tour bus discharged its passengers at the entrance to the shrine, and another came up behind it. The influx of people urged the threesome to move on up to the theater.

Standing on the circular stage, Sarah gazed up at the three massive tiers of seats. It was the most perfectly preserved of Greek amphitheaters, its acoustics unbelievable. A whisper could be heard all the way to the top row, the brochures said.

"Let's climb to the top," she cried, full of energy and enthusiasm for the project. She glanced at her companions, who stood a few steps from her, watching the other tourists as they began to scramble over the marble ruins.

They gave each other a look, then Will shook his head. "My Anna, she cannot climb about like a mountain goat," he apologized. "Her heart."

Sarah was at once contrite that she had suggested the feat. "Should we go back now? We've really seen everything."

"No, you go ahead. We will find a spot in the shade and rest. Then you will join us for a picnic lunch, yes?"

When Sarah looked unsure, they both encouraged her to explore all she wanted.

A few minutes later she was starting up the second tier of seats. She paused and looked behind her, catching her breath. The couple had disappeared, but several tourists were milling about the area, some of them climbing the semicircular rows of stone as she was. Turning, she started for the top.

The third section of marble seats seemed a long way up, she thought as she stood at the top of the second and gazed in that direction. Well, the theater held about fourteen thousand people, so you couldn't expect it to be small, she reminded herself, drawing a deep breath into her panting lungs.

A movement to her left claimed her attention. Two men were moving up, angling over toward where she stood in the midst of the marble benches. They must have been athletes, the way they were hurrying. She spared a second to admire their style before going back to her self-appointed task.

"Sarah."

Her name startled her, a low, tense whisper of sound. But there was no one in speaking distance, much less whispering distance, of her. She glanced toward the two men who had stopped and were gazing downward.

"Sarah, come to me."

Looking toward the stage far below, she recognized a familiar outline. Her heart pumped blood riotously throughout her body. "Mark," she said, a smile spreading over the delicate oval of her face. He had come! He must have seen her note.

Rushing, she clambered down the marble tiers, careful of the chipped edges and bits of grass growing in the cracks. She was entirely breathless when she reached the flat circle of stage.

Mark caught her in his arms, crushing her to his chest as if he would never let her go. "Come on, let's get out of here," he said. Holding her wrist, he guided her from the area, past the entrance where Will had insisted on purchasing her ticket as well as his and Anna's.

"Wait," she said urgently. "I'm with someone."

"Me," he said succinctly.

"No, a couple, Will and Anna Arnheim." She twisted her head in each direction, trying to get a glimpse of them. In the parking lot, the car was gone. She stopped abruptly. "They're gone," she murmured, puzzled. "Without me."

Mark cast her a hard glance before putting her in a small car, slamming the door, and going around to the driver's side. He turned on the engine. "Fasten your seat belt," he advised as they started down the winding road.

She clicked the strap into place, suppressing resentment at his tone. "Why would they leave without me?"

"Have you ever heard of white slavers?" he asked without looking at her.

"I . . . I don't believe that. They weren't," she protested.

"How do you know?" he asked with inexorable logic. "Why did they run out on you, then? Who were those two men who were running toward you up at the theater?"

She remembered the way the two men had been coming up the steps. And they *had* been heading toward her with grim, determined expressions, now that she thought about it. Visions of what she might have escaped paled her face until only her lipstick provided color.

"I trusted them," she said slowly. Her eyes flicked over to Mark as he drove with competence and speed along the road. She saw his mouth tighten, as if with anger. "They were at the hotel in Athens. And at Sounion." She considered the situation. "I don't believe they were anything like that."

His fingers gripped the wheel. "I don't give a damn what you believe. Just don't go off like that again, do you hear?"

"I can do what I want," she told him coldly. "I'm old enough to decide for myself what I want to do."

The car swerved to the side of the road into an old olive grove. Mark cut the engine. Turning to her, he took her shoulders in hands that didn't hurt, but neither were they gentle. In the second before his head lowered, she realized what he was going to do.

His lips covered hers in a kiss that was supposed to be punishing but wasn't. As soon as flesh touched flesh, there was only tenderness.

She understood that he had been worried about her

safety. "Oh, Mark," she whispered as his mouth caressed hers in soft touches that mingled their moistures and turned her lips rosy once more.

"Promise me you won't do anything like this again. I nearly went out of my mind when I returned and found your note. I nearly stole a car," he confessed in rasping tones, dropping kisses along her jaw before moving back to her lips.

"Where were you? You were gone all night." She spoke against his mouth, her breath uneasy in her chest at his nearness.

Slowly he placed her back against her seat. "I had business to attend to." His tone was flat.

In other words, none of her business, she thought, angry that he felt free to do as he pleased but wouldn't give her the same right. She turned to gaze out the window with a little sniff of disdain.

His hands on her shoulders brought her around. "Sarah, you're in a strange country. You don't know the language or the customs. I don't want you to go off without me from now on. Do you hear?"

She hated his manner. "This is my vacation," she reminded him. "When we're in port, I want to go sight-seeing and exploring. You seem to be busy all of a sudden."

"I'll make time to take you around," he promised. "I'm on vacation, too, remember?" His hands caressed her upper chest lightly through her blouse. "You invited me to join you."

"I merely suggested it," she said stiffly.

He smiled. "And I accepted your suggestion. That makes us a team." He raised his hands to her face, slipping them into the hair at either side of her temples. Slowly he urged her mouth to his. His lips barely touched hers again and again. It was as if he were restraining himself from kissing her as he wanted to do, yet he couldn't stop touching her mouth with his in deliciously tantalizing caresses.

"You're dangerous to me, Sarah Lynn Abbot," he whispered. "Dangerous and addictive. Do you know that I want you? I could hardly keep my hands off you in Athens. I couldn't get enough of looking at you."

"I didn't think you noticed me at all at first. I thought you were looking for someone else. Another woman." Her lips met each foray of his between the words they spoke.

Sighing, he released her. His smile was filled with an irony she didn't comprehend. "No, it was you I was looking for. It was always you," he added on a deeply serious note that seemed to relate to some time other than the recent past.

A frisson went down her back as he started the engine again. They were silent on the trip back to the port. The journey to the valley dedicated to the god of healing had done nothing for her except cause confusion, she decided. She didn't understand Mark's attitude. She wasn't even convinced that the Arnheims had meant her any harm. There had to be a logical reason for their disappearance. What if Anna had had a problem with her heart?

She glanced at the man beside her. He had truly been concerned for her. His worry had actually been greater than he had admitted, she realized, remembering the feel of his arms around her and the tension evident in his strong frame as he held her.

Her lips still tingled from his kisses. He had cared enough to come after her. That had to mean something. But what? There was a dichotomy in Mark that she didn't quite grasp; it was as though he had two distinct sides—one openly friendly, and the other deeper, more hidden. Well, she didn't understand him now, but maybe she would before the trip was over.

4

~~~~~~~~~~~~~~~~~~

They're after her," Mark said. He spoke in Greek.

He was talking to Baruch, who, in reality, was Kelly Achinson, his partner in this task. Kelly's Greek ancestry and his fluency in the language, learned from his grandparents, had earned him this particular assignment.

"The question is, who are *they?*" Baruch mulled over the problem. The pitted skin of his face made him look older than forty-five, and his air of competence spoke of long experience. Mark had worked with him once before in Paris.

"What difference does it make? The result will be the same if they succeed: We'll never see her again."

The undercurrents of emotion in the younger man's words, as well as his tense stance, indicated his state of mind. Baruch, leaning against the guardrail near the stern of the ship, cast Mark an appraising glance. He shifted his position as if impatient with his companion's worries. "Maybe you're making too much of yester-day," he suggested.

Mark shook his head slightly as he adjusted his balance to the roll of the sea. The journey to Mykonos had started at dawn, and night would fall before the freighter arrived in port there.

Sarah was still asleep, he assumed. She had gotten angry with him for his probing questions last night after they returned to the ship, but she wasn't the type to stay mad. Remembering his fear for her when he found her note, he was filled with fury, not a hot, unreasoning one, but a cold, clear-thinking anger that reached inside him to some savage instinct for survival that included her in its defense.

He could *feel* danger as if it were a tangible presence. His first partner, a wiry redheaded New Yorker of Irish descent, now retired, had once told him to go with his instincts. "You get a gut feeling that stays with you— believe in it," Donnell had warned him. Mark wished his mentor were with him now. He had the same sense of approaching peril that he had had in Paris one time. He fingered the scar on his wrist, wondering if Achinson would understand if he tried to tell him about it.

Sarah would, he thought. He had to watch himself around her. She was not only smart, but intuitive as well. She already discerned more of his emotions and thoughts than he could allow. It was important to him that she have the carefree vacation that she deserved, not one filled with regrets.

He must control the passion that sprang forth when they were together. He wouldn't use her that way. In his experience, sex had mostly been used as a weapon for seduction and betrayal, revenge and punishment. She would hate him if she thought he'd made love to her as part of his job, and that's exactly what her logical mind would think if she found out the truth.

He sighed heavily. Life was fraught with complications, he thought grimly, turning his attention back to his partner.

"We don't *know* that the two men were anything other than tourists," Baruch persisted. He frowned in concentration as he went over the facts. "Except for what the Brit said. You say he approached you?"

"Yes, he knew me, and he had the correct passwords. He thinks the men are the same two who abducted that diplomat who wanted to defect. The guy disappeared without a trace from a guarded hotel room." Mark grimaced. "And hasn't been seen since."

"Yes, but the men at Epidaurus—"

"Their actions were suspicious," Mark interrupted. "They weren't wandering about the way most tourists do. They didn't stop to look at the sights. All their attention was on Sarah."

"Their methods seem rather inept," Baruch said contemptuously.

"Not if we had bought the story that Sarah had simply gone sight-seeing." The slate gray eyes watched the approach of a cruiser, and Mark relaxed only when it veered off north of them. "They could have taken her up to Corinth and out of the country by air before we knew she was gone."

"How did they know about her?"

"There's got to be a leak in the Company—or two leaks, one back in the States and one in Athens. Particularly in Athens," Mark said slowly, considering the evidence. "Our contact there was the only one who knew our itinerary."

"Anyone could get the ship's schedule."

"If they knew Sarah was on it, yes," Mark agreed.

"What about the British agent, Renfro?" Baruch countered.

"I didn't tell him where we were going when we left Sounion. He was following the trail of two men . . . the ones suspected of abducting that diplomat . . . and it led him right to Nauplia—"

"And they were prepared with a plan to lure her away, assuming the couple were in on the snatch," Baruch finished the thought.

They were silent as each of them considered the implications of these facts. By using a question-and-answer technique with one of them taking the pro and the other taking the con, they worked their way through all the possibilities of the situation.

"How did Renfro get in on this?" Baruch asked, still exploring the involvement of the British operative from Military Intelligence.

"When the two men were spotted in Athens by an MI agent who was on another case, Renfro was called in. His government contacted ours, wanting to know if we had any 'sensitive' people in the area. The Big Boss asked him to get in touch with us."

"What did you tell the girl?" Baruch asked. "How did you explain the couple and the men to her?"

"I said they were white slavers," Mark's reply was curt.

Baruch whistled softly. "Did she believe you?"

Mark grinned sardonically. "Not her. Right now, she probably suspects I'm loco. She's very observant. And with her background, she's bound to have an uncanny ability in deduction. I don't think she'll buy any more tall tales if something else does happen." He frowned thoughtfully. "If something does, we'll have to tell her the truth, or she'll think the worst."

"This job is a lot harder than being a special assistant to the white-glove guys, isn't it?" Baruch ribbed Mark about his regular assignment to the entourage of the presidential envoy to the Middle East. "You didn't know what you were getting into when they asked you to spend your vacation in the Greek Isles."

Mark smiled at his partner's repartee but he was far from amused. Because of his memory for faces, one of his main duties was to watch for known terrorists while escorting VIPs who came to visit the "trouble zones." He also watched for contacts between people in the U.S. embassies and agents of other governments. This was the first time he had been asked to look after a genius who needed a break from routine.

He had liked his duties abroad—until he'd become involved with Sarah Abbot. One of the first things he had made clear to his new chief upon arriving in Paris six years ago was that he didn't seduce women.

"What about the widow?" his boss had asked.

"I meant, as part of a job," Mark had replied stiffly. He should have known no part of his life was hidden from the chief. Nor was his affair a seduction: it was a relationship of mutual friendship and need.

The gray eyes flicked to Baruch, who was absently rubbing his chin, the bantering smile of a moment ago gone. Mark had seen the other agent at several functions he had attended in Paris over the past six years. They had worked together to identify an under secretary who had been selling information from the U.S. embassy in Paris, but Mark didn't know a great deal about the man. Deep-cover agents didn't tell a lot about themselves.

"This Michael Renfro—what else did you find out from him the other night?" he queried, referring to the night that Mark had spent ashore in Nauplia, leaving him the task of guarding the girl.

"Not much."

"What does he look like?"

"A dapper sort of fellow—British tweed and all that—with a bulbous nose that looks as if it's been broken. Do you know him?" Mark asked, noting the rapid blink of Baruch's eyes as he glanced up, then away.

"I might have seen him," he admitted. "What did you two do?"

Mark had to suppress his reluctance to disclose his actions. The questions were beginning to irritate him. "We looked at photos all night, but I didn't recognize anyone. Also I didn't get a look at the faces of those two men at the ruins, so I don't really know if they are the same two Renfro is watching or not. And we don't have a clue to the whereabouts of the Arnheims."

Baruch nodded. "We've broadcast a description of them to our people. All ports of entry are covered."

"Renfro said he would do the same." Mark broke his words off as Sarah appeared on deck. She was wearing shorts and a halter top of white material that contrasted attractively with the golden tan she was acquiring. He couldn't stop the heated response of his body to her. She was becoming necessary to him, he realized.

"I can see I've been supplanted in your thoughts, so I'll go back to work," Baruch said. His quip was lost on Mark, who was already moving down the deck to the shaded area where Sarah was.

That night Sarah was awakened by the vague thump of old tires coming to rest against the wharf. They had reached port after a long day at sea. Lying there drowsily listening to the sounds on the dock as the crew secured the ship, she entertained the fantasy that soon her handsome lover would come to her, make love to her. But he had been more distant with her today than ever before. It didn't take much insight to know that he was avoiding her after those revealing kisses in the olive grove.

Now wide awake, she stayed in bed until all was quiet once more, then rose, slipped into her robe, and went to the porthole. She watched the late rising of the moon and felt infinitely sad. What had she hoped to find when she started on this odyssey? Adventure? Excitement? Love? Passion?

She had found the last one. Whenever she and Mark were together, the fires ignited, but what would come of it?

Closing her eyes, she considered the consequences of this fast but slow journey into the realms of desire. There was a burning, growing ache inside her that demanded appeasement. Mark could give her that. He was the only one who could, she realized. He would be gentle with her . . . loving and kind in his passion.

Her teeth bit hard into her lip as she stilled the tide of longing that rose to unbearable heights. The yearning was more than passion, and she knew it. Pressing an unsteady hand to her throat, she fought an impulse to weep.

If she only let herself love a little bit, then maybe it wouldn't hurt so much when the vacation was over. A summer fling—that was all that they could share. With an increasing maturity, she faced this truth and accepted it.

Restlessly she gazed out at the quiet dock. The moonlight outlined the island of Mykonos in luminous mystery. It was a night for romance. It came to Sarah that she really had found all she had been looking for in life: adventure, excitement, passion, and love.

She drifted outside, lured by the night. The scent of Mark's cigarette came to her from the darkness under the awning. She waited for him to speak, but he didn't.

Emotion began to build in her as he continued to pretend she wasn't there. She walked to the edge of deep shadow, not knowing what she was going to say, but determined to let him know she knew of his presence. "Don't worry," she said coolly. "I'm not going to intrude on your solitude. I just wanted to know if we were at Mykonos."

"Yes," he said laconically.

"Thank you." She retreated to the railing.

He followed her into the moonlight, stopping when only a step remained between them. Sarah's breathing became difficult. She waited for something, she wasn't sure what.

"You should have stayed in your room," he said in a low restrained tone. "It's dangerous to be up and wandering about a ship in the middle of the night."

"You're here," she defended herself.

"And what if I had been someone else? A drunken sailor who got on the wrong ship? Or someone looking to steal something? You're supposed to keep your door bolted at night."

He tried to speak rationally and not antagonize her, but he wanted to shake her until she realized the danger she was in. And then he wanted to kiss her until she forgot everything but how it felt to be in his arms.

"All right," she said quietly, with dignity. She pivoted from him, heading for her room in defeat.

Mark caught her arm, swinging her slender form around until she came up against his hard chest. There she was cradled with such gentleness, she nearly cried. She didn't understand him at all. She sniffed back her tears.

"Oh, Sarah," he said resignedly. "Don't be hurt. Don't you understand?"

She shook her head in the confined space where her

face rested against his chest and his chin touched the top of her head. "No," she choked, "I don't. What do you want me to do?"

His breath was expelled in a low snort. "Don't you know?"

"No," she whispered. She only knew that she was miserable and he was the cause.

"Dammit," he cursed softly. "Don't you know that ever since I kissed you, I've wanted to do it again . . . and again?"

Joy caused her heart to miss several beats, then to bob around in her chest like a cork on the sea. "Oh, Mark," she breathed. "Why don't you?"

He ignored the invitation in her words and her upraised face. His hands held her lightly around her waist, his fingers massaging her skin through the robe and silky pajamas. "Do you think that's all I want? I'm thirty-two years old. Do you think I'd be satisfied with kisses for long?" His hands tightened in warning.

She ran her hands up his arms, stopping at his powerful shoulders and feeling the hard muscles that could so easily hurt her. There was no fear or misery in her now, only a shining passion.

"Make love to me," she said, caught up in the magic and excitement of the moment.

"Sarah," he groaned, "you don't know what you're saying."

A tremor surged through his strong frame, and her arms slipped around him, hugging him close, needing to share with him the wonder that she felt.

As she flowed against him, his arms involuntarily closed around her, and he pressed his face into the soft fluff of curls that smelled of air and sunshine and flowers. Sarah understood at last the strife that had grown between them. The tension of desire as well as concern for her welfare had prompted his actions.

"Yes, I do. I'm not a child."

"I know that," he said fervently. His lips touched her temple, then slid moistly down her cheek. Her mouth was ready when he got there. He kissed her lips lingeringly, his tongue running over the wonderfully soft surfaces in exploratory searches. This was what she would feel like all over, he thought, his senses quickening to a sharp ache at her nearness. "Open your mouth, Sarah." He spoke huskily as she surprisingly resisted his invasion.

"I'm not very good at kissing," she apologized for her lack of experience. He would be disgusted with her.

"Open your mouth. Say 'prune,'" he ordered gently.

As she opened her lips on the odd word, his mouth took hers in a kiss of endless pleasure. She found it was all quite natural, not like the time in college when her first love had snarled that she kissed like an old maid who didn't know what it was all about. That was said after she'd refused to let him copy her lab reports. She had been mortified by his cruelty.

Now she perceived that his technique had been as much at fault as her inexperience. Mark knew just how to guide her with his passion. Her response was as natural as the warm sea kissing the shore.

When Mark released her lips, he drew in a breath like a man starving for air. "Potent," he whispered as he moved to the area around her throat, nuzzling the smooth flesh, biting and sucking in a mood of playfulness.

"I feel so . . . so . . ." She couldn't explain the floating, bursting sensations that filled her trembling body.

"Funny?" he supplied, teasing her with the word she had used the other time she had been in his arms on the deck at night. "You make me feel funny, too."

His hands moved up and down her back, then slipped along the curve of her buttocks to stroke her thighs. They wandered back along her sides, and he pulled her closer until her breasts were fully against his chest. She seemed to be touched all over by him.

His hands roamed over her again, then suddenly he bent and lifted her into his arms, starting down the deck with her pressed to his heart. "Sweet Sarah," he murmured when she buried her face in the curve of his shoulder.

She wanted this night, she realized, no matter what tomorrow might bring. They would have this night.

He carried her to her cabin, turning once they were inside so she could lock the door behind them. Then he crossed the room. Carefully, as he had the day she'd slept on deck, he laid her down. Lying beside her, he covered her legs with one of his. Leisurely he unfastened her robe and eased it to each side. Through the sleek nylon of her pajamas, he explored her body in long, sweeping caresses that left her burning and breathless.

Returning his touch, she placed her hands on his chest and slowly worked the buttons of his shirt free. She slipped her arms around him, stroking along the smooth skin of his back. "You feel so good," she purred in a whisper of happiness.

Mark placed a finger inside the neckline of her top; found that the elastic gave easily. With infinite patience, he pulled the material downward until a breast was exposed, a pale gleam in the darkness. His lips closed over the small rosette, fitting its shape as perfectly as if they were interlocking parts that had been made for each other. His tongue flicked back and forth across the sensitive tip, driving her to gasping madness as her need for him became concentrated in the center of her body.

"You respond so beautifully," he said hoarsely. "So naturally."

His deepened tones were filled with wonder, as if he,

too, were overcome by the surging power that flowed between them. He pressed closer.

She felt the hardening of his body through the nylon and denim that separated them. It gave her a heady sense of accomplishment to arouse him this way. With this man, she was a woman, nothing else, not a brain, not a device, but a person. Female, warm, and desirable.

All that was joyous and loving in her burst forth to bathe him in her fiery passion. He gasped with the strength of it as she moved against him.

His broad hand spread across her belly, adding fuel to the fires that raged there. He pushed her top upward, then slipped his fingers beneath the stretchy waistband. He smiled as she reacted instinctively, pressing against the heel of his hand as he explored freely along the curves and grooves of her soft body.

"Please, please." Her voice faded on a moan of pleasure as he stroked her satiny skin.

"Sarah," he groaned his need. "You're so lovely."

For eternal, passionate moments, they gave themselves to each other. Their lips met; merged; shared heat, moisture, and broken words of praise and longing. Stroking, playful tongues waged mock war; were wounded, revived, given shelter in the other's mouth. There was a fierce, bountiful meeting of skin on skin as his chest sank against her bare breasts.

At last, he pulled back, easing them apart. "I shouldn't be touching you," he murmured.

"Are you being honorable?" she asked, half teasing, half serious.

"Something like that," he agreed.

"Can't you pretend I'm just another girl in another port?"

He knew she was as far beyond his grasp as a distant star, yet he couldn't let her go. His need for her was too great. It isn't seduction this time, he told his conscience. This time it's love.

He slipped his arms under her shoulders and, holding her crushed to him, pressed his face against her neck. His voice came to her muffled. "With you, there can be no pretense. None at all."

She was profoundly moved by his declaration. There was a mystery to the statement. It wasn't a declaration of love, but somehow, it seemed to have meanings even deeper than that often overused word. "Nor for me," she said quietly. She waited, knowing the next move was up to him.

He sat on the side of the bed. Bringing her hand to his lips, he kissed each knuckle, then turned it over and kissed the palm. His tongue explored the exact center, causing a tingling fire to run up her arm. She gave a small unconscious sigh.

"I might not be a very good lover," he cautioned. "It's been a long time since I've been with a woman."

He had gently broken his involvement with the widow upon discovering their affair was known in his department. Now she was happily married again and had two children. He occasionally had dinner with her family when he was in Paris.

"Why is that?" Sarah asked, her curiosity stirred by his confession. It could only be by his choice, she surmised. No woman that he desired would be able to refuse him.

He grimaced, and his eyes went darkly thoughtful. "Meaningless sex doesn't appeal to me, and there's been no place in my life for attachments in . . . a long time."

She wondered about that tiny pause. How long was a long time? What had happened in his life that had made him turn cynical and hard? She experienced a raging jealousy of all other women who had shared his life while she had not. "No women at all?" she asked.

He smoothed the curls at her temple; watched them spring back as if they had a mind of their own. "I was in Paris for a while. There was a widow there. She was my friend, and I trusted her."

"I see." Trust seemed to play an important role in his feelings toward people. What terrible thing had happened to him to disillusion him about life and people?

With caring hands, she smoothed along his shoulders. Spreading her hands over his biceps, she followed the line of muscle and bones to his wrists. She explored the scar on his left arm. Inside, she thought, he was still hurting from old wounds that had never healed. She wanted to make him well. Was her love strong enough?

Her action apparently decided him. Gently he removed the rest of their clothing. His eyes moved over her slender form. "Do you know who Praxiteles was?"

She answered without thinking. "A Greek sculptor who lived around 350 B.C. He is most famous for his marble statues of Aphrodite and her son Eros, known as Venus and Cupid in Roman mythology. He was the originator of the school of art that depicted the female figure with grace, sensuous charm, and nobility of expression." She waited to see how he would take this recitation of facts.

Mark moved closer to her, almost touching so that she felt his body heat radiating over her skin. "He could do you," he murmured. *"The Young Athena. Innocence Personified,"* he suggested the titles.

"I don't want to be any of those things," she whispered wistfully. "I'd rather be your love . . . lover," she corrected. She brought her hands behind his head and, burrowing her seeking fingers through his dark hair, she urged his lips closer to hers.

He allowed his mouth to drop to hers, and then they were caught up in the seriousness of loveplay. His strong body shifted so that they touched all along their chests and thighs. His leg slipped between hers, and hers closed over his. She turned to him.

He was powerful and demanding in his passion, gentle in his strength. His mouth moved over her lips, his tongue joining hers in the game they played. She felt herself filling with a great tide. It rushed in, receded, returned. His body floated against hers, away, then back.

"Mark," she whispered.

"Yes, sweet love?" He nipped with tender love bites along her neck, his hand going to her breast to massage it to fullness.

"Hold me," she said, feeling that she was in danger of being swept entirely away on this magic sea.

His breath mingled with hers when he spoke. "I am, darling, with all my might. Don't be afraid."

"I'm not." She kissed his cheek and jawline, a wildness coming over her, a need to touch him again and again. Her hands stroked his sides, his hips, and slipped over his thighs where the skin was lightly brushed with hairs that had gone almost golden from long exposure to the sun.

Mark had never been so aroused, yet so in control. He schooled his clamoring body to patience. She must always come first with him; her pleasure would always take precedence. He felt her increasing excitement, and his blood urged him toward the culmination.

He teased the smooth inner texture of her lips, liking the feel of it, reminded of other places where her body texture was as smooth and would be as moistly welcoming.

Sarah knew an internal rapture of blazing purity. She

72

was burned without being consumed by the heat of their embrace. Her body moved of its own volition, making its claim on her lover.

"Sarah, I want you," he said in rasping tones.

"Yes."

"But I'm not good enough for you."

"Don't say that," she protested. "It isn't true."

"Yes, it is . . . but maybe it doesn't matter." He sounded sad. "I don't know. I don't know anything except how good it feels to hold you."

She cried his name in little gasps as his hands moved over her slender figure. His touch was familiar to her, not alien.

His hands moved her a little, positioning her so that he could lie over her, his thighs completely enclosed by hers, all parts of their bodies meeting as he held his weight on his arms. They were irrevocably one now. Gently he continued to stroke and excite her until she writhed under him like a flame blown by the winds of love.

Carefully he continued the slow voyage of discovery, reminding himself that this was virgin territory, something as new to him as the act of love was to her. He smiled when she opened her eyes and gazed into his, and his heart ached at the look he saw in their velvety depths. At last, they reached the distant shore.

"A perfect fit," he murmured against her ear, loving the way she had accepted him as part of herself.

"Is it?" she whispered on a panting breath as his hands coaxed her back to the peak of desire.

"Absolutely," he said, hearing the faint note of anxiety in her voice. "You please me." Her hands touched him in gentle ways, and his body answered. "You give me pleasure." His voice was husky, unsteady.

She sighed as if he had praised her extravagantly. A movement of her body urged that he hurry, and he answered her need with that of his own.

They were bound together, magnificent in their passion, and where their bodies touched, their souls met. They gave of themselves, each to the other.

When she opened her eyes a long time later, she turned her mouth to his in a quick kiss of gratitude. Then she smiled slightly, dreamily content with life at that moment.

Mark examined her expression, running gentle fingertips along her lips. "You make me feel so young, Sarah," he said.

"You *are* young."

"Not since I was fifteen," he contradicted. He pulled the sheet over them, and Sarah snuggled against him, her body fitting his perfectly. *Congruity* in all its meanings, she thought, perfect harmony, perfect shape, perfect agreement. He stayed with her until the dawn.

5

~~oooooooooo~~

Morning was almost gone when Sarah finally woke. Her sleep had been deep and peaceful. Dockside noises aroused her curiosity, and she swung her legs over the side of the bed, groaning a little at the stiffness in her body. She hurried to shower and dress and dash down to the galley for some breakfast. Mark was nowhere to be seen. Disappointed, she ate quickly and went back to the deck to look over the new port.

Mark was right on the wharf, watching as Giorgio loaded boxes on a flatbed wheelbarrow. A cat wound itself around his legs.

"Good morning," she sang out, unable to keep from looking at him. He wore a pair of navy blue shorts, but no shirt.

He glanced her way, grinned and answered. "About time you got up. Did you sleep well?" he asked with a wicked leer just for her as he came up the ramp.

"Yes." She dropped her eyes demurely, then immediately raised them again. He looked so incredibly handsome with his smooth tanned skin and straight masculine frame. She couldn't believe that only a few hours ago she had known rapture in his arms.

"Shield your face, young Sarah," he said softly, stopping by her side.

Her smile wavered at his stern tone. "What from?" she wanted to know.

"If you must look at me, you mustn't give yourself away. It's time you learned subterfuge," he lectured her in a low voice. His eyes denied his words as they ran over her in open admiration.

"You're looking at me," she accused.

"A man is allowed to peruse the female population." His smile was sardonic.

Sarah lifted her chin into the air. "For your information, I was thinking of Plato," she informed him loftily.

His slate-colored eyes glinted with laughter. "Plato?" he questioned, a mocking inflection in the name.

She let her eyes sweep over his brawny chest and arms. "That's not his real name. It was a nickname given to him because of his broad shoulders; *Plato* means broad or wide." She couldn't help the triumphant grin that spread over her face. "I was thinking his nickname would do for you, too."

"Oh, yeah?" he challenged, flexing his muscles for her. "What was his real name?" He looked as if he didn't believe she knew it.

"Aristocles. He was named for his grandfather, a common practice in those days as it is today."

Mark ruffled her hair. "You're just full of facts, aren't you?" he teased.

Her lips curved upward. She was so happy, she wanted to dance to a wild bouzouki right there on the boat with him. She looked at him through her lashes, perfecting her innate feminine wiles.

"Sarah," Mark muttered on a sudden rasp of agony, bringing her worried eyes to his face.

With a quick move, he took her arm and pulled her along the hall and inside her cabin. Pushing the door closed behind them, he swept her into his arms, crushing her soft trembling lips beneath his in a long kiss, only to add several short ones when it ended. It was as if he knew he should stop, but just couldn't.

"You make me forget my own name," he whispered, pressing his lips against her temple. "How am I supposed to remember that I shouldn't be doing this?"

"Why not?" she asked, resting against him in an attitude of complete trust.

"Because," he replied enigmatically. "I've got to get out of here." His smile took away the seriousness of the words as he glanced over at her bed.

"Mark," she said, unconscious entreaty in her voice.

He touched her lips, rosy and moist from his. With a careful thumb, he wiped his moisture from her. Then, as if he couldn't control the impulse, he kissed her again. "Do I have lipstick on?"

"No, I didn't wear any today."

Her eyes were shining. Gently he kissed them closed, then he slipped out the door before she had time to realize he was leaving. "Good morning," she heard him say, and Baruch answered in his gruff growl. She waited until the men left, and then she went outside again.

Perched on the railing, she looked over the busy harbor scene. It was like a picture postcard. The land stretched in a broad curve around the bay, rising to rocky hills that weren't as craggy and high as others she had seen in the islands. The town rose up the hillside in a series of white cubes. The people must use whitewash by the ton, she decided.

Fishing caïques dotted the port, their sides low in the water as if they already held their catch. A fisherman in a blue shirt and a black billed cap nodded to her as he worked with a length of rope on his boat. Cats prowled the area, meowing for scraps.

Near the freighter, in an area designated for luxury yachts, a man dressed in nautical whites and blues, obviously the owner, elaborately directed his crew as they put into port and tied up. The captain of the large yacht subtly motioned to the men behind the owner's back, correcting his orders with deft hand movements.

Sarah giggled, then her eyes went wide. "Oh, no," she gasped as the owner turned toward her and she saw his face. She dashed below deck before Sherman J. Sampson, alumnus of Duke University and her scholarship sponsor, could spot her. What ill fate had brought him here at this time? He would ruin her vacation, tell everyone who she was. Her relationship with Mark was too fragile to withstand any sudden shocks.

Walking toward the galley to have another cup of coffee, she stopped in surprise as she heard muted angry voices coming from a nearby room. Quietly, she went back upstairs, heading this time to the port side of the ship. Everything seemed to be going wrong at once.

What had Mark and Baruch been quarreling about? she wondered. Surely not about Mark being in her bedroom. What business was it of Baruch's? She instinctively didn't trust the seaman. Something about him struck her as shady, not quite on the up-and-up. If he was involved in a smuggling operation, and if Mark was in it with him . . . A ripple of concern went through her. Then her logic reasserted itself. Mark couldn't be involved with anything illegal. He was too wonderful for that.

Oh, yes, that's a really logical conclusion, she silently mocked herself. But the very best cryptanalysts were a unique combination of intuition and logic, and she was one of the best. She decided to go with her intuition.

Her worry lifted, and she was able to think about her other problem—Sherman J. Sampson. Well, she would just have to avoid the wealthy industrialist.

Mr. and Mrs. Jeddermann came on deck, and Sarah was pleased to see the frail elderly woman up and about. It seemed terrible to spend a vacation in bed. Unless it was with Mark, of course, she silently added as she smiled at the couple.

She sat in a deck chair and watched the activity around the freighter. It was there that Mark found her some time later. "Come on, lazy bones, I'll take you shopping and then to lunch." He spoke to the captain as they left, telling him of their plans.

Sarah kept her face averted as they went ashore, but no one was visible on the yacht. She breathed a sigh of relief as she tagged along after Mark. Away from the pier, she smiled happily. "We'll be here until Friday?" She asked Mark about the schedule.

"Umm-hmm. Would you like to go over to Delos in the morning? There's a motor launch that goes regularly." He cocked an eyebrow at her, catching her vigorous nod of agreement. "Watch it, young Sarah," he warned.

She tried to bring her rioting joy under control. He really would think she was juvenile if she couldn't do better than this, she fussed at herself. It was just that she was so happy! Giving up, she gave him an impudent grin.

Catching an ancient bus, they rode up the hill from the port to the town proper. A sign over the driver's seat said the fare could be charged to a major credit card. Sarah giggled. The price of the ride was about ten cents. Mark took her to a hotel overlooking the bay where the view was lovely. They ate outside.

"Do you know what Mykonos is most famous for?" Mark asked as a pelican landed on the rock wall around

79

the terrace. He tossed the bird a piece of bread from their basket.

"The windmills?" she suggested, pointing to the thatched roofs below them.

He shook his head. "It's the pelicans." He threw their friendly beggar another crust.

"Why is that?" She hadn't noticed an unusual number of them.

"They're considered a good luck charm by the local people. It's thought that they bring wealth and prosperity to the island. As long as at least one bird stays here, the gods are smiling." His own smile at her was so warm and inviting, she didn't care what the gods were doing, just as long as he continued to look at her like that.

"I see." She dropped her head a little, hiding her eyes from him. She was learning to be more subtle, she thought.

They ate souvlakia, which was lamb, peppers, and tomatoes grilled over an open fire. With wine, fresh bread, fruit, and cheese, it was a perfect meal. Afterward they simply wandered about, looking at the buildings—everything was whitewashed stone, including the walls and windmills.

"Come on," Mark said, pulling her into a shop. "I want to buy you a present."

Sarah tried to tell him not to spend his money on her. "You've paid for everything we've eaten or done onshore. I should buy you something."

"Okay," he agreed.

"What?" she said stupidly.

"You buy me a present and I'll buy you one." His solution was simple. So they each ended up with a gold chain around their neck, a pelican on hers, and the sea god, Poseidon, dangling from his.

Back on the deck of the freighter, they watched a

lone pelican parade about with self-styled importance. The Sampson yacht was gone. Sarah relaxed and smiled up at Mark. Then she noticed that his eyes were narrowed, and he was alertly surveying the waterfront. Following his gaze, she gasped.

"It's the Englishman," she whispered. "What's he doing here?" She looked at her companion. "What do you think?"

Mark was unperturbed. "This is the most popular tourist spot in the islands. Why shouldn't he be here?" He turned her toward her cabin. "Why don't you take a nap? I want you fresh tonight."

"Why?"

"We're going dancing. Dinner and dancing and maybe a little seduction after that," he said, leering at her. His face sobered. "Just kidding."

She could hardly tell him that she didn't want him to be joking. With a wave of longing, she wondered if he would ever turn to her openly, without that shield of restraint she sensed surrounding him.

Going into her cabin, she kicked off her sandals, but instead of lying down, she peeked out the curtain. At the end of the ramp, Mark and Baruch stood talking. When they glanced her way, she shrank into the room. At last, Baruch came aboard, and Mark started off down the street. She watched until he disappeared from sight, going into the bar the Englishman had come out of. Why had he gone there?

Stretching out on the bed, she wondered about the British gentleman. Apparently he was touring the islands on his own. His presence hadn't seemed to bother Mark this time. Only she *had* noted a muscle movement in his jaw for just a second when he had spotted the older man.

A feeling like cold fingers down her spine gave a hint of uneasy premonition. There were things here that she didn't understand, and she couldn't even describe in concrete terms what they were.

First, there was the tension she had sensed between Mark and Baruch; they had quarreled only that morning. Just now, though, they had held an obviously friendly conversation down on the wharf—a fact that seemed to indicate they had nothing to hide. Except Baruch was hiding the fact that he spoke and understood English. And both men seemed to know each other better than was normal for a deckhand and a passenger who had recently met.

Second, for a man so absorbed in his business, Mark was strangely reluctant to talk about it, although he disappeared into his room from time to time to work on reports. He appeared at ease, yet there was a tense wariness in him. He had bribed his way aboard the freighter. Had he done that in order to be with her, or for other less innocent reasons?

He had definitely changed after the Englishman had stopped them in Sounion. At Nauplia, he had stayed out all night, then come after her when she went sight-seeing with the Arnheims—what had happened to *them?*—and tried to scare her with stories of white slavery, but she knew it had been something else that he'd feared. He had truly been afraid for her, but why?

Pressing a hand to her forehead, she considered the possibilities. An idea occurred to her. What if the Arnheims had been assigned to get her out of the way while something illegal was loaded on the freighter? Maybe the whole ship really was involved in a smuggling operation. Guns? Drugs? Maybe the regular cargo was a cover.

That possibility didn't seem likely. For one thing, the Jeddermanns were often around; for another, she herself roamed the ship at will, exploring where she pleased, and no one said a word against it. No, everything came back to Mark, Baruch, and the English fellow.

For instance, she'd noticed that Mark stayed outside her room nearly all the time. And when he wasn't around, Baruch usually was. The British tourist had reappeared, and Mark had sent her to her cabin before leaving the ship. Baruch was right outside. She couldn't get off the freighter without being seen.

She drew a deep, painful breath into her lungs. There was only one other possibility. The three men knew who she was and were either guarding her, or they were supposed to abduct her. She couldn't bear the thought that Mark might be mixed up in something really terrible, whether smuggling or kidnapping.

What if he was? Closing her eyes, she considered the chances of reforming him. Love could change a person. But it wasn't her love that would change him—it was his love for her. If he loved her. What if he had done really awful things, not just smuggling, which was bad enough, but also murder? Not Mark, she protested. He wouldn't! He couldn't!

But what if he had? her mind persisted with the unanswerable questions. Would she still want his kisses? Would she still want his hands, his touch that was so gentle, on her body? She agonized over this, her tender heart searching for solutions with all the soul-wrenching despair of a heroine in a Greek tragedy.

It came to her that a woman loved a man for what he was to her—not for the bad things he had done to others, but for the good things he was to her.

And what was Mark Terrington to her that she should lie here worrying over him? She had no answer for that, either.

Getting up, she went to the porthole in time to see Mark return with a six-pack of his favorite local beer. Her mouth twisted with wry humor. While she had been worrying herself sick over him, he had merely gone out for beer.

Mykonos at night was different from what it was during the day. As a seaport, it was industrious and noisily dignified from dawn until dusk. At dark, it became a sailor's haven and a tourist's rendezvous. A meeting of cultures, Sarah thought, and not always the best parts. She watched a group of seamen trying to pick up some young girls. Several fellow Americans talked loudly while a singer tried to perform.

The music drifting from the bars along the waterfront was haunting, with a forlorn sadness that matched her mood. She glanced at her date with brooding eyes.

Mark was handsome in dark pants and a silky shirt that he'd left open at the throat, revealing the medallion that she had bought him that afternoon. He had taken her to dinner at one of the resort restaurants along the harbor. She had chosen a concoction of seafood served in a tomato sauce and hadn't particularly liked it. Now she and Mark were wandering about town, stopping in any place that appealed to them, listening to the music, having a drink, then moving on.

"Let's dance," he suggested at one of the quieter places.

Going to the floor, they joined the throng of tourists who filled the tiny area. "This is just like home," she said. "So crowded you can hardly move."

"Disappointed?" he asked.

She shook her head. To be with him anywhere was heaven—and hell, she mused. She should never have left the safety of her home. Looking up into his smoky gray eyes, she saw a flicker of worry in those depths.

"What is it, Sarah?" he questioned, holding her tightly against him.

She forced a smile to her lips. "I think I'm homesick."

"So am I," he said slowly. His expression was unreadable.

There was pain in his words. Silently they left the crowded floor and returned to the freighter. On the deck, he pulled her into his arms, and she didn't resist. She felt a need to comfort him, to be comforted by him. It was so strange.

His breath caressed her cheek as he pressed her back against his encircling arm. Ever so slowly, his lips came to hers.

His tongue wandered over her lips, then explored her teeth and thrust gently into the warm honey of her mouth. He took the sweet nectar of her into himself, savoring the taste of her, the incredible softness.

He tried to think of a really good reason why he shouldn't spend the night in her bed. Her education in human sexuality wasn't part of his job, his conscience told him. His arms tightened around her as if he were afraid she was going to be snatched from him at that moment. God help him, but he couldn't let her go.

He thought of a future without her and felt as if he were being torn apart inside. He groaned deep in his chest and buried his face in her sweet-smelling hair.

A sound from the ship's stern caught their attention, and Mark moved to place himself between Sarah and whoever was on deck. Baruch approached them, speaking in a low mutter as he swiftly went by and then disappeared into the shadows. The mood was shattered.

Sarah sniffed the night air experimentally. "Did you see anyone with Baruch?" she asked.

Mark was immediately interested. "No. Why?"

"I didn't think he smoked, but when he passed, I smelled cigarette smoke." She was sensitive to odors, and there had been no mistaking the whiff of pungent tobacco.

"He's probably been talking to the mate or the engineer. I've seen them on deck smoking several times. Come on, you're asleep on your feet." He made the last remark as she yawned. He escorted her to her door, making sure she was safely inside before he went on to his own cabin. In a minute, he emerged, hurrying to the other side of the ship. Baruch was waiting. It was time to report in.

The wind created by the forward passage of the motor launch blew Sarah's curls around madly as she sat on a wooden bench beside Mark the next morning. His arm was around her waist, and she was sure everyone on board was envious of her handsome escort. He was wearing a pair of tan slacks and a royal blue pullover that made his eyes take on a different hue, blue tones mingling with the gray.

Gone was her mood of the previous night. She felt buoyant and reassured this morning. The difference was in Mark. He was open and friendly today as he had been in Athens. They were on their way to Delos, and they had a picnic lunch and all day to do what they wanted.

"Did you ask Baruch about his guest last night?" she asked, not really knowing what brought the question to mind.

Mark glanced at her curiously. "No, I didn't think of it." His eyes narrowed. "Why, is it bothering you?"

"Maybe he had a woman on board," she quipped.

"Not him," Mark said dryly.

She angled her head up to observe the handsome planes of his face. "He doesn't like women?"

"I don't know." He changed the subject. "Here we are." They moved off with the other tourists when the boat docked at the island, the smallest in the Cyclades group.

The rugged land was a mass of granite with a hill near the center. It had taken them only a half hour to reach the island, and they had almost three hours to explore before catching the launch back to the larger island.

"Tell me about Delos," she requested after he swung their picnic bag over his shoulder and took her hand in his.

Lazily his eyes scanned the area, and Sarah had the feeling that he would be able to tell her the number of people around, their sex, and any distinguishing physical characteristics if she asked. He was always more alert than he seemed.

The vigilant gaze fastened on her. "You probably know more than I do, but here is the legend of the island: You remember that Leto was visited by Zeus in the form of a swan, right? Well, Leto got pregnant, and Hera, Zeus's wife, was so jealous that she got Gaea, the earth, to promise not to give Leto a resting place—so Leto gave birth to Apollo and his twin sister, Artemis, on Delos, which was a floating island. After that, Zeus chained Delos to the ocean floor, and here it has stayed ever since."

"You didn't tell me about the Delian problem," she reminded him.

"What's that?"

"Doubling the cube. When there was a plague, the oracle told the people to double the altar of Apollo, which was a cube. The ancient mathematicians had a difficult time with that problem. . . ." She stopped, appalled with the direction her careless tongue had taken. Would he suspect anything from this disclosure? Apparently not, for he continued to talk easily about the topic. He couldn't know about her, she had decided during the night. She was just getting paranoid, that was all.

"Hmm," he said as he considered the solution to the

puzzle. "If they took another marble slab the same size and set it on top of the other, they would no longer have a cube. The sides would be rectangular."

"Oh, that's right," she said as if just realizing this truth. Relieved, she changed the subject.

They strolled along the Sacred Lake, which was now dry. According to the myth, this was the very spot where the twins had been born. Marble lions kept watch over the area, their mouths opened in a perpetual silent roar.

Later they got the motor launch back to the harbor. Seated next to Mark, Sarah thought she had never been so content. There was excitement in her, but it was of a patient nature, as though waiting for the right moment. She realized she had known the man beside her for little more than a week, yet their lives were irrevocably tied together. For only the duration of the voyage? For all time, her heart answered.

Raising her face to the sun, letting the breeze blow her hair every which way, she sighed happily. Mark wasn't dishonest. He wasn't an abductor. There had been too many chances to spirit her away if that had been his intent. And he was too protective to mean her harm. Always he put himself between her and the unknown.

The odor on the sea air caused her to frown. She sniffed once, then again.

"What is it?" Mark asked.

"That smoke. It's the same thing I smelled on the freighter last night," she said, sniffing again.

A man leaning against the railing blew out a plume of smoke, which was wafted away by the wind. Mark got up and went to him. While Sarah stared, the two men exchanged cigarette packs. With a laughing remark, Mark returned.

"What was that all about?" she demanded.

He held out the pack. "A Turkish tobacco, very strong and fairly common around these parts." He lit one and she remembered the scar on his wrist as he did. He blew a streamer of smoke toward her. "Is this the same?"

She waved the cloud away, making a face of distaste. "How can I tell with you blowing it right in my face? I thought it was when I first caught a whiff of it. Now, I'm not sure."

He tossed the cigarette overboard. "It doesn't matter." He shrugged the matter aside.

She giggled. "If you start smoking those at night, then I'll really be able to spot your whereabouts easily." She thought of the night he had been in the shadows and had ignored her. Two days ago. It seemed a lifetime. So much had happened between them, and yet, in some ways, they were further apart. Did he regret making love to her?

"What do you mean?" he asked casually. His words held no particular inflection, and his expression didn't change, but she sensed a difference in him, as if all his faculties had been alerted.

"The other night, that was how I knew you were there," she said, feeling ridiculously shy about bringing up the episode that had ended with them making love.

"Monday night," he said, knowing at once which night she meant.

She licked dry lips. "Yes."

Abruptly he stood, went over to the man, and returned the pack of unsmoked cigarettes. He refused to take his own back. With a motion toward Sarah, he seemed to be explaining something, then he sat beside her once more.

"What now?" she asked in exasperation.

"I just quit smoking." He grinned. "I explained that my woman objected, so I was giving it up." His smile grew larger. "He advised me to beat you and teach you to keep in your place."

"I hope his wife takes a skillet to his head," she muttered vengefully. *His woman.* Was that how he saw her? As his?

"Then," Mark went on grandly, "I explained that you were good in bed and I wanted to keep you happy so that you would let me—"

"You didn't!" she cried, a flood of color pouring into her cheeks. She put a hand over her eyes. "You probably did."

He took her hand, kissing the palm quickly before anyone noticed, except the man with the cigarettes, and whispered, "No, I didn't. But I thought it."

"Oh, Mark." She bubbled with laughter, realizing he was teasing her unmercifully. "Just you wait," she warned of a time when she would get revenge.

"I like to hear you laugh, young Sarah."

"Don't call me that." She wanted him to take her seriously.

His eyes were solemn as he gazed down at her. "I like to. I like to think of you as young and unspoiled. Your face, when we go somewhere, is all shining and full of wonder. As if each thing you see is a new gift."

His voice trailed into silence, and he seemed lost in his own thoughts. She didn't disturb him. She, too, was silenced by his words. Something in his life had been bitter, she thought. Something had hurt him so, he had never gotten over it. She experienced a cold, dread ache in her chest. What if he could never love again? Sadness misted her eyes. How could they ever be more than what they were right now—a runaway girl on a forbidden journey and a mysterious man who might be a smuggler or worse?

"Tears?" he asked, standing and pulling her up as they nudged into port. He touched the corners of her eyes with a handkerchief. "What's wrong?" His eyes were filled with an undefinable tenderness that touched her deeply. He, too, seemed to feel the sadness of a parting that was yet to come.

She shook her head, helpless to explain.

Mark's gaze automatically surveyed all the visible area when they went ashore. A face briefly appeared at an upstairs room over one of the bars. Renfro.

Yesterday when he had gone to the bar, Renfro had met him in the back and told him that the whereabouts of his two suspects had been traced to Bulgaria. The British agent thought this meant they had brought in someone else. Mark did, too. Baruch thought they were making too much of events. He didn't think anyone knew who Sarah was—and wouldn't want her if they did. What did she really know that any other math genius couldn't work out? was his philosophy.

Mark considered his own feelings. Was he acting too much the mother hen where she was concerned? Baruch had hinted that he was emotionally involved and couldn't see the truth. He had suggested that Mark ask for a replacement, since his judgment was clouded by his feelings.

Mark shook his head. Leave Sarah? It was too late for that; had been since the moment he saw her strolling through the Plaka in Athens, an air of freshness about her. Spunky, yet shy. Mature, yet young. That was his Sarah. Each time he was with her, the old wounds faded a bit more. Someday, he thought. Someday.

Taking her hand, he moved off down the pier, seeking a place they could be alone. He saw a bus. "Hey!" he shouted, startling her and several other people around them. "Come on," he said, pulling her after him. They jumped on the bus, and Mark paid the driver.

They rode along the winding hilly road until they

came to another hotel built into the hillside overlooking the sea. There they clambered down, and the bus turned around, heading for town.

"Did you bribe him?" she demanded, a scolding frown on her face at his tactics. He managed to look injured and innocent, which caused her to giggle. But, she admitted, he was a master of control . . . subterfuge. The word shattered the day for her. Deception was another term for it.

"What brought the cloud on?" he asked, perceptive to her moods as no other person had ever been. They were walking down the steps to the beach. Few people were about.

"I was thinking how little we know about people: what they really are, what they want out of life." She waited for his reply, but he was silent.

He led her along the shore to a place where they had to take off their shoes and wade around a rocky point. Then they were on a small beach that was deserted. Waves swept to shore with a steady roar, sounding like the pulse beat of some huge gentle sea creature.

"Let's swim first," he suggested, placing the bag in a shady spot. He began taking off his clothes. "You did wear your suit?"

She nodded. Her eyes roamed the area. "This is a lovely place, Mark." She tossed off her clothes, handing them to him to put on top of their picnic bag.

Islands dotted the surface of the Aegean, forming compelling spots of darkness against the shining mirror of sea that was blue and silver in the early afternoon sun. In every direction she looked, some fanciful bit of enchantment called to her, a siren song of beckoning, whispering of things past and to come.

"Come on." He raced with her into the water, and there they cavorted as if they were the young offspring of Poseidon. They dived, came up, and spewed water from their mouths like magic fountains; then, laughing, they dived again and came up together, their arms entwined, his strong body supporting hers as he stretched into a lazy backstroke that swiftly took them to a partially hidden rock. They sat there resting after their strenuous play. His hand shook water from her curls.

"My grandmother used to take a pair of scissors and curl ribbon to go on Christmas packages. Your hair curls just like that," he said, pulling a strand straight and releasing it to spring back into its spiral.

Sarah pulled her knees up to her chest. "You've mentioned your grandmother before. Did she live with you?" Her head tilted upward in a sideways glance at him. To her surprise, his face changed, assuming a guarded frown.

"No. I used to visit her in the summer while my parents went on vacation. She lived in a small farming community and taught ballet to the farmers' daughters. She smoked cigarettes through a long holder that she used as a pointer in her classes."

Sensing that these memories were connected to the unpleasant past for him, Sarah brought in a light note. "And what did you teach the farmers' daughters?"

His hand stroked her bare back. "Not as much as they taught me," he quipped, grinning at her disbelieving face. "Ready to eat?"

Leisurely they swam to the sandy apron of beach, side by side, matching stroke for stroke. Their eyes met and held, then their bodies, as they waded to shore.

"I think you're hungry for more than lunch," he murmured, kissing along her temple and licking the saltwater from her cheek.

Her arms closed around his lean waist. Paradise, she thought. Why couldn't it last forever? But nothing did.

She could only love him for the rest of her life, not a moment longer, she mused wistfully. How did he feel toward her?

The thrusting power of his body pressed so intimately to hers told her that he wanted her; the look in his eyes said he had tenderness for her. But there was something inside that held him away, an invisible barrier that only he could see, that only he could cross. She would have to wait for him.

What if he never came to her?

Her arms tightened at the thought, then she stepped back from him. Smiling, she said she was ready to eat.

They settled in a spot below the rocky promontory where there was a little shade, and ate pita bread stuffed with olives, tomatoes, and thin slices of meat. They drank warm beer. After the brief meal, they lay down for a nap, keeping close to the rocks whose shadows shielded them from the sun.

Sarah savored the feel of his body next to hers for only a few minutes before she went to sleep. It was late when she woke. The afternoon had drawn a longer shadow over them, protecting them from the fiery rays of the sun. It was the last day of the month, she realized. Memorial Day? She smiled. It was a day *she* would remember.

Turning onto her side, she gazed at Mark. Even in deep slumber, he had an alert quality about him. He looked younger now. The faint lines around his eyes and the one across his forehead were smoothed by his repose. She wondered if he dreamed.

Yearning to touch him, she dug her hand into the fine-textured sand, letting it run through her fingers in a thin stream. There were infinite grains of sand on the beaches of the world; there were the same number of heartaches, she was discovering.

A finger touched the corner of her pensive mouth. Mark moved over to her. With no teasing or hesitation, his lips fastened on hers as his arms drew her against his warm body.

A devouring hunger gripped them both. With a swift movement, he turned her so that she was positioned under his hardening form. Carefully he eased his weight over her, resting on his elbows while rock-hard muscles pushed against his tan skin as if seeking a way to move closer to her.

Her eyes gleamed as she looked up at him. "Mark," she whispered, wanting him so much.

His mouth devastated the skin along her throat, causing her to writhe beneath him. His small gasp of pleasure wasn't lost on her. She stroked his back persuasively, sliding her hands under his bathing trunks to continue the massage along the hard flesh of his hips.

With firm steady pressure, he moved against her, bringing the spiraling heat from deep inside her until she was consumed by the flames of their passion.

"I need you," she whimpered brokenly. "So much. I was afraid . . . that you didn't want me."

"Never that." His fingers hooked under the strap at her shoulder and slowly brought it down her arm. When her breast was free, he gazed at the small globe as if he had found a rare treasure. His eyes left her to scout out the beach and the visible area of sea. Nothing in sight. They had been undisturbed here for hours.

Blood flooded the turgid lines of his body. He wanted to take her now, without interruption, while she was ready for him. His hand moved down her side, found the edge of the bathing suit.

Sarah opened her mouth as he returned his lips to hers. Her tongue sought the intimate touch of his, accepting it just as her body accepted his caresses. He groaned her name in rising need, unable now to stop the tide that swept them into the churning sea of passion. Only her refusal would halt the flow.

She seemed to become fluid against him as she let herself melt into his embrace and conform to his strong planes and grooves. "Oh, love," she murmured as he moved slightly from her.

"Wait," he said with a deep timbre in his voice. He reached for the bag.

A pelting of sand and stones struck them from above. Three youthful faces peered down at them from the high rocks. The boys shrieked with wild laughter, calling down taunts in Greek. When Mark stood, they dashed off toward the other beach and the stairs that would take them to safety in the hotel.

Mark's glance went to Sarah. Her eyes were averted as she pulled her strap up so her breast was covered.

"I'm sorry I put you in a position like this," he apologized.

She rose and placed a hand on his arm. "It wasn't your fault. I mean, I was hardly an unwilling participant." Her smile was strained as she tried to hide her embarrassment. She had gone into his arms so easily, and it was becoming increasingly obvious that he didn't really want her.

"It won't happen again," he promised, furious with himself. Gathering their things, he handed over her clothes, pulling on his while she did the same. In a few minutes, they were ready to leave.

She looked once at the rocky promontory as they climbed the stairs to catch the bus back to town. It seemed as if the gates of paradise had closed behind them.

"I don't give a damn if you're sleeping with her, but we're supposed to be—"

"Just what is the problem?" Mark asked coolly, interrupting Baruch's low tirade. "I've kept her busy and happy with sight-seeing and excursions. That's what our directive was: Let her have her vacation and get her home safely."

"I think we should put her on the next plane back to the States. Then we can get on with our real jobs," Baruch grumbled. "This isn't my idea of fun."

Mark grinned. "Why not? Here we are, touring the Greek Isles, all expenses paid. Anyone else would give an arm for this assignment. Why not enjoy it?"

Baruch raised one brow. "I'm not getting the same benefits from it that you are."

Ignoring the innuendo, Mark continued, "There really hasn't been anything of a threatening nature, if you discount the Epidaurus incident as a sight-seeing trip and nothing more. I haven't seen anyone I recognize and neither has Renfro. Did he have further information on the Arnheims?"

"How should I know? No one tells me anything. I'm just a deckhand."

"You haven't seen him?"

"No."

Mark was surprised. "I guess he hasn't gotten word, then." He yawned and stretched mightily. "I've got to get some sleep."

"Yeah," Baruch agreed caustically.

Mark spared a moment's sympathy for his partner's boredom with this assignment, then he went to his room. It was after midnight and he was tired. Today had been a strain in more ways than one.

As a precaution and for his own peace of mind, he went by Sarah's door, checking to see that it was locked. It was. He stood there a minute, listening to the silence, imagining how she looked in her sleep . . . wishing he could go in to her.

His face hardened. He wouldn't subject her to any more words like the ones the boys had used for her. Thank God she hadn't understood the language. His insides twisted in loathing at the thought of any smut being attached to her. He wouldn't let her be hurt because of the passion he could arouse in her. He would control it, he vowed.

6

Michael Renfro stood a foot from the window, watching the harbor scene below. A large luxury yacht was easing into a berth. Behind him, looking over his shoulder, Mark glanced at the activity of the busy port, too.

"Tomorrow's Friday. You leave in the morning?" the Brit asked.

"Yes."

"What's the schedule?"

"We're supposed to go to Crete after a brief stop at Santorin to off-load some supplies," Mark replied.

The older man pulled the shade down over the open window, then, as an added precaution, pulled the dusty drapes together. Going to a rickety table, he turned on a low-wattage lamp, whose dim glow went with the general shabbiness of the room. The two men sat in the chairs that flanked the table. Picking up a pack of cigarettes, Renfro offered one to Mark.

"No, thanks. I've quit." A grin briefly touched his lips.

"A noble achievement. I haven't the fortitude." Renfro lit up a mild brand with a charcoal filter.

Mark swallowed the last of his coffee and set the cup aside. He yawned hugely. "I'm tired," he said. "When this case is over, I'm going to sleep for a week."

Michael's glance was sympathetic. "Is it your client or your boss who's keeping you busy day and night?" he asked jokingly.

The muscles in Mark's face hardened perceptibly, and Michael got the idea that this subject was off-limits. His slight smile disappeared, and he studied Mark thoughtfully.

Mark stared, unseeing, at a strip of peeling wallpaper. He hadn't been able to sleep last night and had finally gotten up and sat in the dark hallway near Sarah's room. "Baruch said you hadn't contacted him," he remarked, stirring out of his introspection. "No word on the Arnheims?"

"Yes, as a matter of fact, there is. They appear to be on the up-and-up. The husband is a government clerk, and the wife does have a minor heart condition. They're from Svilengrad."

"That's in Bulgaria, isn't it?"

"Yes."

Mark's eyes narrowed, and his face looked dangerous. "They told Sarah they were from Austria."

"They're not," Michael said firmly.

"The two men you suspect?"

Michael mashed the cigarette out. "They crossed into Turkey, apparently with fake passports, then hired out on one of those floating fish-processing plants. We're still tracking them."

"We?" Mark's tone was sardonic.

"A friend of mine, that is. Actually I'm on vacation."

Mark's thoughts quickly ran in several directions. If Renfro was on vacation, then he was staying in the area because he was interested in this case . . . in Sarah. But the man was too professional to ask what was so "sensitive" about her.

Since the Arnheims had lied to Sarah, that meant they had had something to hide. The sight-seeing trip had been part of a plan to take her. This news would hurt Sarah if she ever learned of the couple's deception. She had trusted them.

His eyes went bleak. Sarah trusted him, too, and nearly everything he had told her about himself had been a lie. Grimly, he returned to the problem at hand. "Things seem okay at the moment. Why doesn't it feel right?"

"Yes," Michael agreed, lighting up another cigarette. "Why doesn't it?" Their glances met in mutual understanding.

Mark went to the door. He listened for a moment before opening it and stepping outside. He returned to the wharf. Sarah was off on pursuits of her own; Baruch had the task of following her.

Mark was deliberately avoiding her, putting distance between them. Last night at dinner and this morning at breakfast, he had tried to return to the open, friendly manner of their first day in Athens. His actions had hurt and confused her, but she had adjusted well, hiding her feelings behind a brave smile that was just a bit forlorn. Well, he thought, a little humiliation now would save a lot later on. He had nothing to offer to a person of her caliber.

He must protect her from her own desire and inexperience as well as his own passion. What was this trip to her but a flinging off of restraints, a time to explore and find out something about life and her inner self?

Having had her forbidden taste of freedom, she

would go home and marry some college professor who was several years older than she, but close to her in mental ability and background. The man would take pride in his priceless jewel of intellect. They would have two children and live in a brick house. That would be the best thing for her.

Mark's jaw clenched into a rigid line. That professor would never know the real Sarah. Not as Mark knew her. He would never know the warm, passionate woman who was capable of so much feeling, who had responded to his touch with such shining rapture that even now he could feel the glow of it, could see it in her eyes as she lay beneath him and looked up at him with complete trust.

His breath hardened in his chest into one gasping pain of longing. He had no right to her, no right at all, but that didn't stop him from wanting, from wishing, or from dreaming.

Sarah was nervous. Her hands were clutched together in her lap, and her tea was getting cold in its cup. Mr. and Mrs. Sampson of Raleigh, North Carolina, were urging her to reconsider their offer.

"You can fly down and join your cruise in Crete," Mr. Sampson said. "There's an air shuttle several times a day, I'm sure."

His wife seconded his idea. "And you'll have more fun with the young people at our villa than you would poking along on a voyage."

They obviously didn't entertain the notion that Sarah was on the freighter because she wanted to be alone. But did she? Now that Mark was so distant with her, life on the ship had lost much of its appeal. The prospect of his chilling friendliness in that confined space for the next four or five days was dismal.

"All right, if you're sure it won't be too much trouble, I'd love to come with you." She accepted their invitation. "I'll have to notify the captain and get my clothes. . . ." Her voice trailed upward in a question.

"We'll help you," Mr. Sampson promised. "In fact, why don't we go do that right now, and then we'll be ready to cast off. I've finished my business here in town."

Before Sarah could say another word, her host gave instructions for one of his men to accompany Sarah and himself to the freighter to pick up her luggage, and they were off, waving good-bye to Mrs. Sampson, who was staying on the yacht. Sarah felt slightly dazed at the turn of events, but with a determined set to her lips, she decided this was for the best.

She had forgotten all about Sherman J. Sampson until an hour ago when she had come face-to-face with him and Mrs. Sampson in a tourist shop in the heart of town. She had been browsing alone among the souvenirs, and they had insisted she come with them for afternoon tea on their boat before they returned to their villa on the other side of the island. Upon learning that she was on her own, they had invited her home with them.

Mark was on the deck, sitting on the railing near her cabin when she and Mr. Sampson went up the ramp. "Did you buy any priceless artifacts?" he teased, coming to his feet as they approached.

"No. Did you get all your reports read?" she asked pointedly. Without waiting for his answer, she asked if he had seen the captain.

"He's onshore, but I think he'll be coming back soon." The gray eyes settled on Mr. Sampson. Mark held out a hand. "I'm Mark Terrington," he introduced himself.

Gritting her teeth, Sarah introduced Mr. Sampson, saying she had known him and his wife for years, and explaining her plans to visit with the Sampsons at their villa.

Mr. Sampson enlarged upon her statement. "She was the most brilliant student my company ever sponsored. In fact, she was the smartest student ever to attend the university, according to my friend, Paul Fielding. He's a professor there, you know," he said confidentially.

Sarah excused herself and went to her cabin to pack. Behind her, Mr. Sampson continued with her life story. It didn't matter now, she thought, wondering what it was about her that turned men off. Was it her mind or personality or body . . . or the entire package that was her . . . that offended the male population? She was pensive as she unlocked her cabin door.

What was she supposed to give—or withhold—in dealing with the opposite sex? She could share her mind, as she did in her work, but she wouldn't let her intellect be abused, as it had been by men who'd wanted her to cheat on exams or reports. With Mark, she was willing to share the pleasure of their lovemaking without making other demands on him. Didn't he realize that?

She paused in her packing. There was no denying Mark's response to her touch. Together, they were a volatile combination. It was something in himself that held him back. What? Some other woman that he loved? The widow in Paris? She would probably never know, for he kept those parts of himself carefully hidden from her. She closed her luggage and went back on deck.

Mark smiled at her when she stopped beside him. "Have a good time," he advised. "We'll see you in Crete in a few days. I know you'll have a better time at the villa than on this old tub." He suddenly looked lonely and bored.

Sarah felt a stab of conscience. She had suggested the trip, and now she was running out on him. Mr. Sampson had the answer to her dilemma. "Why don't you come, too?" he said. "That way, it'll keep our numbers even."

"Why, thank you, sir. That's generous of you." Mark's manner was totally sincere. "Why don't you two go along since Sarah is ready? I'll pack and meet you in about fifteen minutes."

Little more than an hour later Sarah was unpacking her clothes in a luxuriant room of gleaming marble, adorned with colorful wall tapestries and handmade rugs. She had the feeling she had somehow been taken, but she wasn't sure just how. Instead of getting away from Mark, she would be trapped with him in this place that looked like something out of the *Arabian Nights* for the next four days.

She dressed in a flowing silk caftan of blue and gold that she had bought in Athens and hadn't yet worn. She posed this way and that in front of a floor-length mirror to check its effect. When she went down to the terrace a few minutes later to meet her host and hostess and the other guests, she was glad she had worn the outfit. The other women looked like Greek goddesses to her.

Mark, handsome in a light summer suit, was talking to two of the three single women who were present. Mrs. Sampson introduced Sarah to Kit and Pet, saying they were the children of old friends. Pet was short for Petula.

"And if you call me Petula, I'll hit you," the lovely young woman with the lively manner and sexy voice said with a tinkling laugh. She gave Mark a sidelong glance, and Sarah thought she probably wouldn't mind if *he* called her Petula.

In addition to the three single women, there were three single men plus two married couples. Everything nice and even, as Mr. Sampson had said, Sarah thought without much humor. She wished she hadn't come.

"Did you have old Weatherspoon at school?" the man in front of her asked, a twinkle in his eyes.

Sarah searched for the man's name. Daniel something-or-other was the best she could do. So much for her great memory. He must have gone to the university, too, to know the teachers there. "For trigonometry? Yes."

"I had him about twenty years ago," Daniel continued with a reminiscent smile. "He had a mind like a computer when it came to solving math problems, but he never knew whether it was raining or snowing outside."

Sarah noted the wings of gray in Daniel's hair. That plus his statements put his age at about forty. He had tanned skin and a fan of lines around his eyes, and looked as though he spent a lot of time outside. Probably plays tennis, she thought. He was lean and fit.

They were still talking when dinner was announced. She looked around quickly and saw Pet hanging on Mark's arm as they went in the broad doors of the dining room. Daniel offered his arm to Sarah, and she gratefully accepted. She sat beside him at the table.

"You said that you were in communications equipment?" Mr. Sampson asked Mark during the meal.

"Yes," Mark answered. He told them the name of his company and gave a brief history. "It was an established name and I had the inheritance from my grandmother, so it seemed like a good deal to buy it out and then turn it into the type of business I wanted."

"I've heard of the company," one of the married men said. "It has a sound reputation."

Sarah listened avidly and knew a sense of pride in

Mark and his ability to mingle easily with this group of wealthy businessmen.

"I'm having trouble with my radio," Pet quipped. Her smile was seductively sly. "Maybe you can fix it for me?"

"I'll bring my repair kit and have a look at it later," Mark said lightly. He returned her smile.

There was general laughter at this bit of byplay, and Sarah forced herself to join in. Mark belonged with these people, she fully realized. He could talk business and indulge in witty social chatter with no trouble at all. Obviously he was exactly what he had claimed to be all along.

For the rest of the meal, Daniel talked to her quietly. Sarah found him to be an engaging companion, and their talk was interesting. It occurred to her that, while she wasn't a sparkling wit, she could converse on many levels, and other people seemed to like to talk to her. That realization made her feel more secure in this elite company.

Coffee was served in a combination den and sitting room. Along with expresso, a waiter brought in a cart containing bowls of melon pieces mixed with strawberries, grapes, and fresh figs. Plates of cheese, crackers, and pats of butter accompanied the fruit. The guests were told to help themselves.

"I don't know how I'll be able to go back to the humdrum meals I fix for myself when I return home," Sarah confided to Daniel as he handed her a dessert plate. He took one for himself and proceeded to load them both with the treats.

"I know what you mean," he agreed.

"You are a smart one," Pet said in an accusing voice to Sarah as she and Mark stopped by the cart. She poured a cup of hot milk and added a dash of the espresso for flavor. "Imagine thinking of taking a cruise on a freighter to meet handsome men. The idea would never have occurred to me." She gave Sarah an impish grin, then eyed Mark with a blatantly come-hither glance.

She's lively, flirtatious, good-natured—all the things a tired businessman would probably want in a wife when he came home at the end of a hard day, Sarah thought with a kind of fatalistic acceptance. Since joining this company of bright, interesting people, Mark had withdrawn further and further from her. It was as if that wonderful night on the freighter had never happened.

"I'm afraid you give me too much credit," she said aloud, forcing a congenial smile to her lips. "I had no idea who would be on the ship."

"Then it was an act of fate that brought you here," Pet said, speaking directly to Mark this time.

Before he could reply, they were diverted by a suggestion from their hostess that they get up some card games. Pet quickly declared herself and Mark to be partners. Sarah decided she would rather look over the selection of books that occupied one wall of the den, and Daniel stayed with her. At eleven, she excused herself and went to her room for the night. Mark barely looked up from his cards.

Sometime after midnight, Sarah got out of bed and opened the door to the terrace. Silently she went outside and stood next to the balustrade. On a path below her, outlined in moonlight, she saw a figure, and she recognized Mark's swinging stride and broad shoulders. He was dressed in dark pants and shirt, and he was moving swiftly toward a secluded garden that hugged the steep hill between the house and the cliff. From the dark came a tinkling laugh, which she also recognized.

Going into her room, she closed and locked the door

and then climbed back into bed. She had never felt worse in her life.

Mark stood on the decking built at the edge of the limestone cliff. At one end of the platform, stairs dropped almost one hundred feet to the boathouse below. The Sampsons' yacht was anchored there, as well as a small power launch, a sailing pram, and two rowboats with auxiliary motors. The only other access to the villa was by a narrow winding mountain road. Too long and too slow, he had decided, for a quick getaway. If trouble came, it would be from the sea, and that was the way it would depart . . . with Sarah going, too.

He walked back up the twisting trail to the house, aware that he was cutting through multiple alarms. The security guards at the villa knew who he was. There were times when an agent had to trust someone, and he had decided to confide his problems to the head guard and get his cooperation. Mark smiled, remembering how eager the men had been to be in on the operation. Their job consisted mostly of fishing guests out of the swimming pool, he suspected.

Sunday morning, Sarah sat beside the pool. Her legs dangled in the warm water as she rested. She and Daniel had played tennis that morning, then eaten breakfast on the terrace, read the *Herald,* and, since no one else was about, had decided on a private swim meet. He had won all their races in spite of handicapping himself by using only one arm for swimming. Now he was slowly finishing his workout by swimming laps while Sarah watched in admiration.

Out on the lagoon, she saw the sailing pram turn, its colorful sail fluttering, then catching the breeze again as it came back toward the boat dock. In a few minutes, Mark came along the flagstone path to the pool and sat down beside her. Neither of them spoke.

Finally, "Did you enjoy your sail?" she asked.

He nodded, his eyes on Daniel as the older man completed another lap.

Daniel would be good for her, Mark thought. Better than a professor who might have a twinge of professional jealousy for her intellect. Daniel wouldn't. He was a successful man and a mature one. Sarah wouldn't have to worry about things like cooking and cleaning if she married him. He would have servants to look after her every need. And he would probably be a good lover and husband to her. Yes, it would be better if she married him.

For the past three days, Mark had carefully stayed out of the way while observing the growing friendship between Daniel and Sarah. He had managed to convince himself that he was acting on her behalf. Turning, he looked at her quickly, noting the careful smile on her soft lips and the opaque expression in her eyes. She had learned subterfuge, he thought. None of her innermost feelings were visible in her face anymore. For a long, painful moment, he fought the urge to take her into his arms and kiss her until the mask was torn from her and she lay heated and breathless beneath him.

No, it was better this way. He got up and went to the room that housed the security equipment and spoke to the guard there for a time. Then he went to his room to get ready for the party that was to be held that afternoon.

Sarah sat very still after Mark left. She felt as though she were holding herself together by an act of will. The dull throb of a tension headache was still with her, unrelieved by her vigorous activity. She watched absently as Daniel climbed out of the pool and toweled dry.

He came over and sat where Mark had been only moments before. When she glanced up at him, he bent his head toward her, and she prepared her lips for his kiss. The caress was light but lingering.

He had kissed her last night for the first time. Standing at the door to her room, he had taken her into his arms as if she were extremely fragile. She appreciated his gentleness.

From his window, Mark watched the couple at the pool. He had witnessed their kiss last night, too, and had spent a restless night because of it. When they drew apart, Daniel stood up and held out a hand to Sarah. Together they disappeared into the building, and Mark went into his shower.

"I didn't realize there would be so many people," Sarah said to Kit and Pet later that afternoon. The three women sat at a table with a striped umbrella shading them from the sun.

"Oh, they're like flies gathering at a picnic," Pet exclaimed. "Somehow word gets around and all the tourists on the island show up." She was good-naturedly contemptuous of the guests milling around with drinks in their hands, talking and laughing loudly.

At a long table near one end of the pool, the caterers were busy replenishing the food trays and punch bowl. Mark and Daniel loaded a serving tray with tall glasses of wine punch and brought it over to the women's table. There was a scuffling of chairs as seats were rearranged, and Sarah found herself sitting between Mark and Daniel.

As she reached for her glass, her arm accidentally brushed Mark's as he did the same. A frisson went through her entire body, almost as if she had been stabbed. She forced her breath into a slow, normal pattern while her heart rioted in her chest.

One perfect night, she thought. If she lived to be a hundred, she would have one perfect night to remember out of 36,525 nights.

"What are you thinking?" Mark suddenly asked, his voice quieter and deeper than usual.

"About the number of days in a hundred years," she said.

Pet started laughing. "I wondered what geniuses sat around and thought about; now I know."

A blush crept over Sarah's face, even though her laughter joined with that of the others. "Yes, and I do multiplication tables instead of counting sheep to go to sleep," she jested, adding her own humor to the conversation. For the first time, she found she could joke about her mind and not be apologetic for her way of thinking. It was one of many new things she was discovering about herself on this trip. So many new things, she mused, and was a little saddened by the thought.

Her eyes went to Mark, and she found him watching her with something like understanding and pity in those gray depths. Her face hardened slightly. She didn't need anything from him, especially pity.

She wondered if he had slept with Pet. Every night she had locked both the inside and outside doors to her room. Not that she thought he would come sneaking down the hall or along the terrace to her, but . . . Her mind stopped short of thinking about the actual possibility of his coming to her. Would she let him into her bed again? *Yes.*

"Mark?" Pet repeated his name with a sharper inflection.

Sarah glanced at him and saw he wasn't listening to the other woman's chatter. His eyes were roaming over the crowd with a lazy manner that was entirely deceptive. She knew he was intensely alert. Following his line of sight, she looked at the people gathered around the table of food. There was no one there that she knew. Who was he looking for? Mentally she shook her head. He was the most perplexing creature!

With a mumbled excuse, he got up and left the table, still not acknowledging Pet's bid for his attention. Sarah felt sorry for her. Perhaps she should have warned the saucy young woman that Mark was unpredictable. That he could make love to you and then act as if he hardly knew you. No, it was none of her business, and Pet wouldn't thank her for the advice. Putting a smile on her face, she listened to Daniel tell a long amusing story. The afternoon drifted into evening.

The guests showed no signs of leaving as night fell. They danced and talked and ate for several hours. Sarah was tired and wanted to go to her room. Her tolerance for people and conversation had been exhausted long ago. Finally, with half the night gone, the Sampsons cordially called an end to the festivities and sent everyone home. The villa settled into sleep.

Back in her room, Sarah dressed in jeans and a black T-shirt. She put a black scarf over her head and waited, sitting in the dark until all was quiet, then she went out on the terrace, closing her door silently behind her. With a heaviness of heart, she wandered along the steep trails of the hillside garden until she came to the observation deck. There she sat on the railing and watched the blinking lights of a ship near the mouth of the lagoon and contemplated life.

Freedom was an illusion, she realized. She would

never be free of what she was—a mathematical whiz. It was part of her, like her brown eyes, and had to be summed into the total person that she was. Her hand went to the gold pelican hidden beneath her top. There seemed to be so many parts of her that no one wanted. The well of love in her heart was full to overflowing, but no one needed her love, not really.

Suddenly the night exploded into muffled sounds behind her.

"We've had several false alarms," the security chief explained to Mark. "I think someone wants us to think that a small animal has gotten inside the walls and tripped them." His face was serious, but his eyes were lit with excitement.

Mark pushed back his nagging sense of danger and went over the facts calmly. "Where were the alarms triggered?"

"Along the north wall, on the pool terrace, and in the garden going toward the deck. Your man is near the pool."

"None were tripped on the steps from the lagoon?"

"No."

Mark frowned. He had been sure they would come from the sea. "I'm going down to the deck. Your men are all in place?"

The security chief nodded.

Slipping from the room, Mark went along the terrace to Sarah's room. Automatically, as he did every night, he tried her door. It opened. He stepped inside. The moonlight fell across her empty bed.

Gone! She's gone! The words hammered through his veins as he sped along the downward path to the sea. He'd contacted Michael Renfro before; now the man joined him at the pool to follow at his heels. Their steps on the sandy path were swift but silent. Just before they reached the platform, they came upon two figures moving cautiously through the dark.

"Find Sarah," Mark said to Michael as he faced off with the intruders. Michael didn't hesitate to obey. Leaving Mark to hold them off, he ran on down the path to the deck. Behind him, he heard the first thuds of flesh hitting flesh. He ran out on the deck as Sarah whirled around.

"It's all right. Don't be afraid," he assured her. He held a gun in his hand.

Sarah recognized the English tourist at once. Somehow she knew this involved Mark, but she didn't know how. If Mark was in danger, if the Englishman was after him, she would warn him off even if it meant her own life. She faced the man bravely.

"What is it? Who are you?" she demanded.

"A friend," he answered. "Mark will be along shortly."

The sounds of the scuffle increased, and men's voices were heard speaking in low, tense tones. Then the night was eerily quiet. A man came out of the shadows onto the decking.

"Mark, look out!" Sarah called. "He has a gun."

"Oh, sorry," Michael said, putting the weapon out of sight.

Sarah felt like an absolute fool as Mark came forward and the two men talked. She listened, finding out that there had been two of *them* and that the guards were taking *them* down to the jail in town.

"Who were they?" she asked.

There was a fractional pause. "Burglars," Mark explained. "What were you doing out of your room at this hour?" he asked, peering at her in the moonlight. There was a gun tucked into his waistband.

There was more going on than these two were admitting, she realized; then she made the connection. "The men from Epidaurus."

"I told you she was bright," Mark drawled to the Englishman.

"Who are you?" she demanded.

"Michael Renfro," he introduced himself.

"And you? Who are you, Mark? In real life, who are you?"

"I think we'd better go in. This might be a long session." Turning, he led the way back up the path. When they reached the terrace, he went directly to her door and held it for her, then closed it behind them. Michael Renfro had faded into the night; they were alone now in the privacy of Sarah's bedroom.

Mark considered her expression for a long time while he debated with himself on the best tack to take with her. She'd hate him no matter what he told her, he thought. He decided on the truth.

"Sarah," he began gently and saw her flinch. The destruction of her trust in him was the hardest thing he had had to do in a long time. To hurt her caused an equal pain in himself. Forcing the words to his lips, he continued, "I know who and what you are. I know what you do, everything. I have from the first day."

She just stared at him, admitting nothing.

He felt a glimmer of admiration for her stubborn silence. With a grim smile, he reeled off names for her. "Dr. Fielding. Jennifer Westlake. Raleigh, North Carolina. Washington, D.C. The Pentagon."

She was visibly shaken by his disclosures and groped for the bed, sitting down heavily on it. "How do you know all that? Who are you?"

Her wary eyes took in the stranger who stood in the middle of her bedroom. She knew his passion, she thought, but not *him,* the man behind the physical desire. And yet, in her heart, she would have sworn she knew him well—at least, all the important things about him.

He hesitated, then, "I'm assigned to the Middle East, to the staff of the envoy there," he explained. "I was supposed to be on vacation, but I was asked to help look for one runaway genius—"

"You're with the State Department?" she broke in.

"No, I'm with Central Intelligence," he admitted. "When they found out you weren't on the dude ranch where you were supposed to be—"

She interrupted again. "How did they know I wasn't there?"

"Your boss needed some information. When he called, he found you wouldn't return his messages, so he sent someone out to check on you. The girl you hired to take your place confessed to the deception, and Jennifer Westlake disclosed your travel plans. Achinson and I were dispatched to the area to find you." His smile was nostalgic. "You were a shock. You didn't look anything like your picture."

No photograph could pick up all the bright golden highlights in her honey-brown hair, he thought, or the expressiveness of her delicate features, or give a hint of the softness of her lips, now pale and clamped together into rigid lines of control. He had never felt so tender toward her.

"Where're your glasses?" he asked. "I've worried about your falling off the ship or over a cliff without them."

"I'm farsighted. I only wear them for close work, usually when I'm at the computer monitor." She brushed this aside as unimportant. "Who is Achinson?" she demanded.

Mark spread his hands in a gesture that said it didn't matter. "Baruch. He's my partner, a Company man, same as I am." He glanced at her to see if she knew the nickname for the agency. She did.

"I heard him speak English," she said slowly. "That first night on the freighter, after you sent me to my cabin, he came aboard and I heard him say something to you in English. And what's even more ironic is that I once hit upon the truth, that you might be here to protect me, but I thought I was just getting paranoid because of the Arnheims and the Englishman." She had to ask the next logical question. "Then, after you found me, what were you supposed to do?" Her eyes never left his as he considered his answer.

Finally he admitted, "Our orders were to let you have your vacation and see that you returned home safely afterward."

"You were to watch over me?" She wanted to be sure she understood.

"Yes."

"And the Englishman?"

"He's a friend."

"The Arnheims?"

"We're not sure about them," he said slowly. "But they've gone home."

"Were the two burglars really the two men from Epidaurus?" She asked the questions one after another, determined to find out everything.

"Yes."

She looked past him to the window. "Did you talk to Dr. Fielding?" Her voice seemed to belong to someone else.

"Not directly. I did see his report, and he took your side in this whole matter. He advised the State Department to let you have your fling. . . ."

118

Dammit, he swore to himself as a brief flash of emotion shimmered through her eyes. That was definitely the wrong word.

Sarah was stunned at this disclosure. Dr. Fielding had been her mentor and guide for as long as she could remember. For him to bare her soul to others seemed the worst form of betrayal. She would never again be so trusting. Her eyes went to Mark.

"Was taking me to bed part of your job?" she inquired softly. "Did the doctor suggest that, too?"

"Sarah, no," he denied, knowing he wasn't going to be able to convince her differently of his part in the deception.

She stood, her slender body straight and proud. "Was there a summit meeting on the subject? I can see it now—Dr. Fielding, the secretary of state, the head of the National Security Council, maybe even the President—each of them agreeing that Sarah Lynn Abbot should have her vacation in Greece; oh, and did anyone know of a handsome lover who could satisfy her unfulfilled libido? Fortunately, someone did, so it was all settled."

"It wasn't like that," he contradicted her sharply. He came to her but stopped when she stepped back from his outstretched hand. He dropped it to his side, feeling a despair that matched hers. She didn't want his touch; would never want it again. Just for a second, he let himself remember that she had stood on the deck, facing a man with a gun, and had called out a warning to him; then he pushed the memory ruthlessly aside. That was the past; this was now.

"Making love to you wasn't part of my job. I felt guilty as hell for it, but . . ." His voice dropped to low, intimate levels. ". . . but I couldn't resist."

"Well," she said at last, as if he hadn't spoken. "I've

had my vacation and my fling, so I may as well go home. I can take a plane back to Athens tomorrow . . . today." It was almost morning, she realized.

"You'll have to stay in Greece for a few days. You may be needed for questioning."

"Oh." She hadn't thought of that.

"And you haven't seen Crete or Rhodes," he reminded her. He went to the hall door. "You've paid for the full tour." He looked at her for another minute, then he went out, going down the corridor to his own room. He heard her door lock behind him.

Sarah locked the terrace door, too, and slipped out of her clothes and into her nightgown. She lay in the dark and stared at the ceiling for a long time. She had reached the end of her journey, she thought. Her destination had been Hades.

7

But what were you two doing out at that hour, that's what I want to know," Pet teased, her jealousy carefully hidden beneath the friendly banter.

Sarah wasn't fooled, and she doubted anyone else was. She suppressed her irritation with the remark. "I didn't know Mark was there until I heard all the noise," she confessed honestly. She followed Mark's example and made no mention of Michael Renfro, who had disappeared as if he had never been.

The story given out by the guards was that Mark had surprised the two burglars hiding in the garden where they were waiting until everyone was asleep. Fortunately, because of that afternoon's party, the security chief had posted additional men that night and therefore there had been plenty of help in the vicinity to aid Mark.

"I understand that the men managed to get themselves hired by the caterers, and so came in with them, but how did they plan to leave? It's a long walk back to town." Daniel, seated next to Sarah, looked as if he had his doubts concerning the truth of the tale.

"By sea," Mark replied easily. "There was some kind of ship near the mouth of the lagoon."

Sarah remembered seeing the blinking lights out there.

"Well," Mr. Sampson said with satisfaction, "this should be a warning to others. With those two in jail, the local riffraff will think twice before attempting something similar."

The story of a burglary simplifies things, Sarah thought. Luckily, Mark and Renfro, and even the so-called thieves, hadn't used their guns, so the actual scuffle had not drawn an audience. That way no one had to know about Renfro, Mark didn't have to blow his cover, and the nature of her work was still a secret. All was taken care of, neat and tidy.

She refrained from looking at Mark. She felt humiliated, even though she had prepared herself to face him calmly and with dignity. But nothing could erase the knowledge that she had practically forced herself into his arms on the freighter that night. There was, or had been, an attraction between them, but Mark wouldn't have acted on it if she hadn't gone to him. She wondered if he hadn't felt mostly pity for her. Anything but that, she silently pleaded.

Daniel looked at his watch. "Almost two o'clock," he said. "How about a sail in the pram?" The invitation was for Sarah.

She stood. "How about a peaceful ride in a rowboat? Sailing sounds too strenuous for me today." She took Daniel's hand and they left the terrace.

Mark took a drink of coffee without really noticing what he was doing. Sarah hadn't once looked at him since she had come out of her room shortly before noon. He wished he had never agreed to come on this trip and that Sarah was safe and snug in her own apartment several thousand miles from here. He was haunted by the thousand-and-one frustrations that beset a man when he gets entangled with a woman. If only he hadn't made love to her, then maybe his longing for her wouldn't be so fierce, so persistent.

His attention was riveted on her as she left with Daniel. He tried to think of something that would entice her to stay.

Well, hell, Terrington, he scorned himself, why don't you just throw yourself in front of her? He got up and walked off without even realizing Pet was talking to him.

"I'm sorry. What did you say?" Sarah glanced at Daniel as she bent to her oar. She hadn't heard a word he had said for the hour they had been out on the lagoon, not even when they had stopped rowing and watched the sea life in the depths of the clear water.

"We'd better head in," he said gently. "Sarah?"

"Yes?" She really looked at him this time.

"You leave in the morning. I fly back to the States the next day. I'd like your address and phone number. I want to see you when you get back."

The seriousness of his request couldn't be ignored or turned aside with a flippant answer. "I . . . I don't know," she said, confused as to whether she wanted to see him again or not. She wasn't sure it would be fair to him.

"There's someone else, isn't there?"

She shook her head.

"There was, then. But if that hasn't worked out, I'd like a chance."

"Daniel . . ."

"I'm forty-one, Sarah. I know what life is all about. I'll give you three months." He paused and considered. "Well, two months, I promise. Then I'm going to call and ask you out to dinner. Don't make up your mind until then. Will you promise me that much?"

Slowly she nodded.

Several people arrived at the villa after dinner that evening. The Sampsons were giving a farewell party for Mark and Sarah, and it was turning out to be a quieter, more intimate affair than the one of the previous day. Sarah thought three or four parties a year would be plenty for her. She decided she would go to her room as soon as it was decently possible.

Across the large room, Pet's tinkling laughter drew her eyes that way. She clings to his arm as if she'd been superglued on, Sarah thought in disgust. Surely he's getting tired of all that giggling and pointless chatter by now. It was about to drive *her* up the wall.

Remembering his words about a roaming man having few friends, Sarah revised her assessment. Pet exuded warmth and good cheer. He probably loved it. He *obviously* loved it, she amended. He had stayed with her every waking minute . . . and sleeping one?

At this thought, Sarah experienced such a rage that she actually wanted to throw her punch glass at the laughing couple. She was amazed at herself, and stopped to examine these new emotions. She sounded just like a jealous shrew, she realized.

And she had no right to. Mark had never promised her anything. Now that she understood the basis for his withholding himself from her, she felt guilty about her own part in their affair. It was his job to stay with her, and she had made it impossible for him to refuse to sleep with her.

Daniel touched her arm. "Come on. Let's dance."

They moved to the end of the room where other couples were slowly swaying to the music from the stereo. Mark and Pet joined the group.

Pet beamed a bright smile at Sarah from her position in the warm circle of Mark's arms. In that instant, Sarah decided that no one, especially those two, would know that she wasn't having the time of her life. She grinned impishly and deliberately stuck out a slender foot as if to trip them. Giggling lightheartedly, she spun away from Daniel, executed an intricate step and danced back into his arms.

Taking his cue from her, Daniel began a complicated series of steps that she followed inexpertly but gamely. Soon they had created a riot on the floor. The other dancers started showing off, too, and there was much laughing and switching of partners back and forth. Sarah found herself in Mark's arms. He two-stepped her over to the shadows.

"I've never seen you like this," he said. He looked as if he disapproved of her flirtatious actions.

She gave him an innocent, wide-eyed look. "No, you haven't." She dropped her lashes demurely, then spun out of his arms and back into the middle of the floor, where Daniel caught her.

Later while having a glass of icy fruit punch she saw Mark go out onto the dark terrace, Pet clinging to his arm as usual. The bright remark she had been about to make faded from her mind, and she was filled with acute misery. She was no good as a social butterfly, she mused unhappily. It was a pose that was too hard for her to maintain.

"Shall we go for a walk?" Daniel held out his arm.

They walked down the garden path to the wooden decking over the cliff. Below them, the dark waters murmured moodily against the rocky precipice. She sighed.

"I wondered how long you were going to keep up your front," Daniel said. There was kindness as well as amusement in his voice. "It's Mark, isn't it?"

She couldn't answer.

"Is this the first time you've been in love?" he asked.

"The second. Both of them miserable," she confessed. She had *thought* she was in love that first time, so it didn't matter that she knew now that it had been nothing more than infatuation.

"At the risk of sounding like a Dutch uncle, would you mind if I said that things will get better as you get older, or maybe I should say, easier?"

"Will they?"

"Yes," he assured her. He smoothed back a curl blowing across her temple, and she remembered Mark doing that. "You're such a sweet . . ."

She thought if he called her a child she would scream.

". . . feminine type of woman. It makes it hard for a man to be around you."

"What do you mean?" That was the strangest statement she had ever heard.

"You're very desirable, but a man feels compelled to protect you, even from himself."

"I . . . well, I . . ." She didn't know what to say. Was that the way Mark felt, too? A tiny ember of hope flared inside her. "That was a nice thing to say, Daniel. Thank you." Rising on her toes, she kissed him on the cheek.

"Ready to go in?"

She shook her head. "Would you mind if I stayed here? I'd like to be alone for a while." Her smile gleamed in the moonlight. "I think my people quotient is about used up."

With a touch and a murmured good night, he left her and went back up the path. Sarah turned to the sea, watching its movements, trying not to think or feel. She glanced up once when Mark came out on the deck, then returned to her contemplation.

He said nothing, only stood several feet from her and waited. Later when she turned to go back to the villa, he fell into step immediately behind her, following her to her door.

There, Sarah faced him, and they gazed into each other's eyes for a long moment. Flitting thoughts raced through her mind. She felt she should say something to him, but she didn't know what. Turning, she went in, closed and locked the door, then listened as he checked the knob to be sure that it was secure.

"Good night, Sarah," he called softly through the portal, and her heart gave a lurch of surprise.

She immediately started analyzing that gently worded good night as she prepared for bed, but she gave it up while brushing her teeth. Who could ever understand men?

The shuttle flight over to Crete took off at seven the next morning. It was only three-quarters full, and the passengers looked grumpy and sleepy, Sarah thought. She looked out the window as Mykonos fell away below them, and watched the changing colors of the sea as the sun played on its surface.

A flight attendant offered them fruit and crackers. Mark took an orange, but Sarah declined anything.

"The freighter isn't due until evening," he said, peeling the orange and tossing the peels on a plastic tray the attendant had placed on the drop-shelf in front of him.

Sarah was aware of his gaze on her and of the brooding look in his eyes. When she glanced his way, she carefully looked no higher than his chest after one searing contact with his eyes that left her trembling inside. "Yes," she murmured.

"What would you like to do today? We could go sight-seeing," he suggested. "Knosós isn't far from Hērákleion."

"I thought . . ." Her voice was raspy. She cleared her

throat and tried again. "I thought I'd see about getting a flight out tomorrow, first of all, then I'd . . ."

"A flight to where?" he demanded.

She didn't like his attitude. "To Athens, of course, then home," she replied coolly.

He frowned heavily. "No." He bit angrily into a slice of orange, then swallowed, hardly aware of what he did. "I mean, you haven't seen everything yet."

"I thought I would go sight-seeing today, after I made arrangements for the flight. Alone," she added.

"You can't go alone."

"The men have been caught. Surely there's no danger anymore."

"Maybe there is, maybe there isn't." He shrugged. "But you can't go off on your own. I have to stay with you."

"Because it's your job," she said.

"Yes." He knew what she was thinking. "But it wasn't part of my job to make love to you. I don't operate that way." His words sounded stilted, and he groaned inwardly in frustration.

"But it was my fault that you did," she admitted. "I practically forced you to."

"Hah!"

His scornful exclamation needed no other disavowal, and he made none. She glanced at him in uncertainty, and his eyes met hers in steady denial of her words. She looked away.

"You . . . you didn't really want me."

"You know better than that," he said softly. A finger under her chin turned her face to his again. Her eyes searched his, and he saw the tiny flicker of hope in their velvet depths.

Leave her alone, the voice of his conscience advised. What did he have to offer her, anyway? He had no money other than his salary, a small savings account, and a few investments. He had no settled home to take her to, no friends or relatives he wanted her to meet. He had nothing to give her but himself.

"Did Daniel ask for your address before you left?" he forced himself to ask her.

She nodded, waiting. Everything in her seemed to be waiting for something. She wasn't sure what. Or if she would want it.

"Did you give it to him?"

"Yes." Why was he torturing both of them this way?

"He seems like a steady sort of person . . ."

"Oh, Mark," she whispered in despair and turned back to the window.

He finished the orange and wiped his hands on a napkin. He was silent as the flight attendant came by and picked up the small tray. For a long moment, he stared at Sarah's averted head, then he reached out and stroked through her curls. "We could rent a car, go sight-seeing, and stay someplace along the coast tonight," he said. "Just the two of us. Would you like that?"

She went very still, then she turned, her eyes searching his again. Was he serious? "What about Captain Theodopoulos?"

"We can leave word with the port authorities that we'll rejoin the cruise tomorrow."

"No." She shook her head. "It's impossible."

"Why?" he asked softly.

"Because it just is. I don't feel the same now."

"Why?"

She couldn't answer. Inside her, a storm raged, destroying logical thought. All she knew was that she wanted whatever he wanted. Her spirits began to climb like a kite on a strong breeze.

"I want to be your lover, Sarah, but I won't beg," he said. He grinned at her, and her heart melted. "Though

I think I'm willing to do even that. Please, darling Sarah, come with me." He was teasing, but serious, too.

"I . . . all right," she heard herself say. She had to drop her gaze for she couldn't stand the sudden flame in his eyes.

"Oh, love, you are so new and enchanting," he whispered. "But you do know what you're doing, don't you?"

Her hand reached out to him and was clasped by his. He was being honest with her. He was telling her that this was merely an interlude, nothing more. She could accept that. "Yes, I know."

He insisted that she consider her actions carefully. "I'm offering you nothing but myself. A person like you, Sarah, deserves more than that."

"Oh, Mark, that isn't true." Her arms went around his waist, and she pressed her face to his chest.

He pulled her close. "I only know I want you more than I've ever wanted anyone in my life." His kiss sealed the promise in his words.

They were told to prepare for landing, and Sarah, with Mark close beside her, watched Crete come into view.

To the southwest, Mount Idhi rose in snowcapped splendor more than eight-thousand feet above the sea. Along the coast, plains were intersected by rocky promontories that gave the island a rugged, crenellated outline. This land would always hold a special place in her heart, Sarah thought as they dropped toward the tarmac.

A daydream began to take shape in her mind, one that involved her and Mark, and a home in the States . . . and maybe a garden, and children to play in it. She realized what she was thinking. Don't, she told herself and meant it.

After the plane landed, Mark and Sarah left their

message for Captain Theodopoulos, locked their bags in the trunk of a small rental car, and started off on their journey. First Mark drove her around Hērákleion, the capital city of Crete.

To Sarah, the town seemed both quaint and gaudy. The tourist industry was obviously a big part of the economy. Travel agencies and car rental offices dotted every corner, it seemed. But then, a square would contain a stone fountain with scalloped edges and lions holding a huge marble bowl on their heads, and she would be delighted. Vendors crowded the streets in the tourist sectors, offering items from foodstuffs to "genuine" Greek antiques.

"The price of civilization," Mark commented.

"Yes. Oh, look," she · said, pointing to a Greek Orthodox priest dressed in flowing black robes, wearing a shortened version of a chef's hat and sporting a bushy white beard.

"Impressive." Mark flicked her a glance, taking in her bright eyes and flushed countenance. "You look like a kid going to a party," he teased.

She saw him frown slightly as he spoke, and some of her joy gave way to apprehension. He really wasn't all that sure about this, she thought. There was still something that held him back in spite of his avowal. But what? Was it his past that troubled him? Or was there someone he had loved, perhaps still loved, who haunted his present?

"Why so solemn?" he asked, lighthearted again.

She was startled out of her introspection. "No reason," she replied. "Look at that sign." She pointed out the road sign. "I thought Knosós was spelled K-N-O-S-S-O-S."

"It used to be, but the government changed it to one S in the middle."

"Why would they do that?"

"Who knows? Maybe some misanthrope in the road department did it to confuse the tourists."

"I can believe that!" she said. They laughed together and the tension between them disappeared. "How far to the ruins?"

"About four miles."

In a few minutes, they were parking and paying the fee to go inside. The path was dusty, for the summer months were the dry season on Crete, but trees shaded the area, surrounding the level upon which the ancient palace stood. On one side of the ruins, the land rose in gentle foothills; on the other, it fell into the shallow water of a creek. Other ruins at the site included the remains of noblemen's houses that cozied up to the perimeter of the palace grounds.

They wandered about, admiring a wide expanse of stairs leading to an upper room and columns that were smaller in diameter at the bottom than at the top and stained with terra-cotta.

"There's no maze," Sarah complained. "And no Minotaur."

"Unless you count the palace itself. It's pretty confusing," Mark noted as they came to a dead end and had to backtrack through a passage that kept veering off in one direction, then another.

They stopped in front of a wall mural.

"See the double ax?" she said. "It's called a *labrys,* and the palace may have been called *labýrinthos.* Ergo: labyrinth." She laughed up at him, pleased with her deduction.

"That was very astute. I never thought of that and I knew the word for ax, too."

"They loved color and texture, didn't they? And beautiful paintings." Sarah fell silent for a moment.

One wall contained two scenes, one above the other,

depicting servants wearing short skirts, ankle and arm bracelets, and carrying vases, probably filled with wine and sweet oil, she assumed. "Even the servants had painted toenails," she commented, pointing this out for Mark's benefit. He grunted, definitely unimpressed. "Nice-looking young chaps, don't you think?" She waggled her brows in a ribald manner that brought his arm around her in a tight squeeze.

"I like the way the women dressed back then," he said.

"Yeah, topless," she agreed wryly, catching on right away to what he meant. The sense of timelessness that came to her each time she visited one of the ancient sites erased the humor and left her with a pensive countenance.

"What are you thinking now?" he asked softly.

"That if we had lived back then, I would have brought wine to you and washed your feet when you returned home and anointed you with sweet oils. I would have served you pomegranates and passion fruit and grape leaves filled with meat and cheese."

Her voice was very low, like a melody heard from a distance and carried on the evening breeze. His eyes kindled as he gazed down at her upturned face. There was a look of rapture about her, as if she saw far visions and knew runes and magic. His heart beat so hard, he thought it would leave his chest.

"And then?" he asked, afraid of breaking her spell.

"Then I would have sung you songs of conquest and songs of love and played on the lyre while we watched the gathering of evening by the old gods until the sun was swallowed by the sea."

"And?"

Suddenly she seemed to realize what she was saying. With a trembly little laugh, she exclaimed, "Oh, we would have thought of something to do after that. Just don't expect any hot meals. I'm a lousy cook."

"I'll handle that part," he promised solemnly.

Turning, he guided her along hallways and across galleries until they came to a rectangular porch with three of its terra-cotta columns still intact and supporting a protective roof.

"The Minotaur!" she said with a throaty cry of delight.

Mark looked pleased, as if he had given her a much wanted gift. They silently admired the mural of a bull whose head was lowered and hooves positioned as if he were charging an unseen opponent. His shoulders were massive and his curving horns sharply pointed.

"For you," Mark said in a voice deep and huskily fierce, "I would slay beasts." His hands cupped Sarah's face, and his thumbs massaged along her cheekbones.

"Would you?" she whispered, her eyes quietly serious.

"Yes. I would fight monsters and I would destroy evil in order for you to be safe."

"And then?"

His face softened. "Then I would come home and eat the fruit and drink the wine . . . and taste of the honey that is you."

He lowered his head, and his mouth took hers in an endless series of kisses that were barely touches of their lips but promised of kisses to come when evening arrived and they were alone.

Sarah sensed an awareness of him building in her; she knew he felt it, too. It was a swelling sensation, like the growth of the flowering bud of a rose, which would first bring forth beauty and then its reward, the seed.

A sigh lifted her small bosom, causing his darkened gaze to sweep over her with a possessive gleam.

A tour group caught up with them, a smiling, talkative

bunch of Scandinavians who crowded up to the guard-rail where they stood.

"Come on, sweet maiden," Mark whispered in her ear.

Holding hands, they ran from the area in a light-hearted spirit of adventure, dodging broken columns and skipping along the many stairs until they had left the lovely crumbling stones behind.

"Hungry?" he asked as he started the car and backed out of the parking space.

"Starved." Her eyes glowed, watching him while he guided the compact vehicle along the winding road.

"You're blinding me with your brilliance," he complained, shielding his eyes with a hand as if he couldn't see to drive.

"So squint," was her mocking advice. She laughed when he pulled his sunglasses off the sun visor and stuck them on his nose.

They stopped at a taverna and bought flat barley bread and souvlakia, putting the two together into a sort of sandwich. The side order of *kalamaria* looked like fried onion rings but was really fried squid, which had been pounded until it was melt-in-the-mouth tender. For dessert, they had the honey-and-nut pastry, baklava.

Eating outdoors in the shade of a sea pine, with a row of stately Italian cypresses behind them, Sarah thought she had never been so happy. The taverna was on a rocky promontory jutting out over the sea, facing the north.

She watched the roll of a small wave on a tiny patch of beach below them. "What kinds of tides do they have here?" she asked.

Mark took a swallow of beer before answering. "Not much of any," he explained. "The Mediterranean is too small to be affected by the moon and the sun."

"Oh." She lapsed into silence again as she thought that over. The moon would have the most influence because it was the closest, and the force of attraction was inversely proportional to distance. Her velvety brown eyes went to her companion. The closer she was to him, the more she was attracted. And also, the longer she was around him, the more she wanted him. Then, too, the more kisses she received from him, the more . . .

"What are you grinning about?" he suddenly demanded. "I haven't seen an expression like that since my dog chased a neighbor's cat into the fish pond when I was about eight years old." He tweaked her nose playfully.

"I'll tell you tonight," she said, trying to look mysterious.

"Oh, like that, is it?" He stood. "Come on, love. Let's get on down the road."

Returning to the car, they drove east on the coastal road with its spectacular view of bays and coves and beaches. Sarah found herself gasping with awe every time they rounded a curve. An hour later, they reached the end of their trip.

The hotel complex that Mark had decided upon was on a large bay a few miles beyond the town of Ayios Nikólaos.

"Ayios Nikólaos," she mused. "Doesn't that mean . . ."

"Saint Nicholas," her escort supplied.

She remembered that he had said her curls reminded him of Christmas ribbons, and she smiled.

He glanced at her. "I'll have to remember that you never forget anything."

The hotel sat on a promontory overlooking the bay. The entire complex was a miniature Greek village complete with a tiny blue and white chapel, a taverna, a café, an art gallery, and more.

Sarah's eyes swept from one thing to another as she tried to take in everything at once while Mark signed them in. Glancing over his shoulder, she saw that he'd listed them as Mr. and Mrs. Mark Terrington and wondered about their passports. He talked to the clerk in Greek, and both men laughed and looked at her. She gave them a bright grin.

In a few minutes, they were following a bellboy who escorted them to their bungalow, which was set among some carob trees below the main building. Stairs were built into the cliffs, connecting the bungalows and two semicircular beaches to the top of the headland.

In the room, their guide importantly showed them the amenities of the suite, which could rival those of any Continental hotel. He showed them the shower and bathroom, how to adjust the air-conditioning, and the refrigerator hidden in a cabinet. He kept glancing at Sarah for her approval and she kept nodding and smiling and murmuring "Yes . . . yes . . . lovely . . . yes, thank you" while stifling her impatience for the young man to be gone.

"There's wine and beer and bottled water as you requested," he said. "Everything is chilled. The fruit." He pointed to a basket on a low coffee table in front of the settee. "There are crackers and cheeses in packages."

"Thank you. I'm sure we can find what we need," Mark spoke up. He handed the younger man some money and ushered him out the door, closing it firmly behind him..

Sarah found that her breath had completely disappeared as Mark slowly turned to face her.

His slate-colored eyes ran over her small figure, burning her with his longing. Her blood began a pagan beat through her veins like ancient ceremonial drums calling the villagers to some dark ritual. When would the rites begin? she wondered.

"Well, Sarah?" he said.

8

~~~~~~~~~~~~~~~~~~~~~~~

Whatever you're asking, the answer is yes," she said.

Their eyes feasted in the honeyed glances they exchanged, and she felt that his gaze penetrated her barriers and freed the woman she was meant to be.

"That's what I like about you, Sarah Abbot—no coy acts, no social innuendo, no blushes, just truth and honesty." His expression became thoughtful, and when he spoke, it was as if the words were addressed to himself. "And yourself, freely given."

"Well," she said shakily, "you don't have to take me."

He laughed softly at that.

But she was serious. "When this is over, when we part, then let there be no regrets and no hard feelings. Whatever we share now, let it be apart from all else, a moment taken from all time, and ours alone."

"No strings?" he questioned.

"No strings," she affirmed. She wanted him to know that he was completely free of any commitments to her.

He came to her.

She closed her eyes as his arms slipped around her slender body and enfolded her to his chest. She felt his lips on top of her head, pressing kisses into the halo of curls again and again. Then he roamed down, seeking her lips with his, not really kissing, but touching in brief intimate contacts that left her warm and strangely satisfied as if a hunger for sweetness had been appeased.

"Shall we go for a swim?" he invited.

"Yes," she murmured, opening her eyes as he released her.

"You take the bathroom," he said softly.

"That's all right." Opening her carryall, she took out her swimsuit and then undressed and put it on, leaving her clothes scattered over the oversize bed.

Without seeming to notice her, Mark did the same. He laid his shirt and slacks over a chair, then gathered her things and put them there, too.

"You're very neat," she commented, frowning slightly. "I tend to leave everything where it falls when I take it off."

"You probably haven't lived alone as long as I have. When I get ready for bed, I don't want to have to find it under the debris." He grinned and gave her an oblique glance. "Come on."

They swam in the large pool and then had drinks in the shade of a carob tree. Sarah was totally aware of Mark.

"Did you know the carob is also called the locust or Saint John's bread?" he asked, gazing at the lacy foliage above them.

"Umm-hmm," she said, bemused by her own heightened emotions. "The seed pods are edible and are reputedly the locusts and honey found by Saint John in the wilderness. Tons of them are exported as cattle

140

fodder. The seeds were the original carat weight used by goldsmiths." She sipped dreamily from the crystal glass of iced fruit punch. Everything in her was waiting . . . waiting.

"Wow," he breathed softly.

"I have a mind like a trashcan," she apologized. "It's full of useless bits and pieces."

He shook his head, refusing her apology. "I like it."

Sarah looked at him solemnly, wondering if he really did, or if it was part of his job to say so. She put the thought from her. *No regrets, no hard feelings.* She had made the rules; she would have to live by them.

When he held out his hand, she accepted it, letting him pull her to her feet and guide her along the steps to their bungalow. He insisted that she take the bathroom first, so she bathed and perfumed and rubbed lotion into her skin, which was now a lovely shade of dark gold.

While he showered, she sat on the bed in her robe and towel-dried her hair. When he came out of the bath, she slowly laid the towel aside, not noticing that it dropped to the floor.

Her eyes enjoyed the sight of his male leanness as he came toward the bed, covered only by the white strip of towel around his hips. He was wonderfully handsome —tanned and healthy and strong in his manliness.

"Do you want to rest for a while? Take a nap?" he asked huskily.

Her eyes answered for her. When he chuckled, she broke into an open, happy grin, then flashed him a provocative glance from under her lashes.

His face became stern. "Excuse me, madam, but do you have a license for practicing wiles?"

"Oh, uh, yes, but I left it in my other purse," she said, giving him a mock anxious glance.

"Well, I suppose we can let it pass this time, but . . ."

His voice left off teasing as he reached a hand out to her. He sat on the side of the bed and slowly gathered her into his arms.

Sarah felt the trembling ripple that went through him, and she slipped her arms around him, tilting her head back in order to make her lips accessible to him. His mouth closed over hers.

This time he didn't nibble but partook of the entire feast. His tongue traveled a deliciously lingering route over her bottom lip and then the top one. He stroked inside, following the line of her teeth, finding the invisible nick on the bottom tooth and rubbing back and forth across it.

"You have the softest lips," he told her. "And the sweetest."

She pressed tiny kisses to his throat, feeling the pulse beat with the tip of her tongue, then exploring along the strong cords of his neck. His lemony after-shave teased her, and this time, there was no odor of tobacco to interfere with the scent that was uniquely his.

He rose, bringing her to her feet. Leaning over the bed, he stripped the covers back and pushed the four fat pillows into a mound. He turned to Sarah.

She watched as his hands went to the sash of her robe, and his eyes questioned her for permission. She nodded. Deftly he untied the belt and pushed the garment from her shoulders, letting it fall in a heap next to her towel. The towel from his hips joined the group.

With gentle touches, he came to her, melding them into one body, one passion, one plateau of ecstasy, and as they climbed ever higher, his strokes quickened and became urgent.

"We must be approaching the speed of light," she gasped, straining upward to meet his every movement. "Time is slowing down."

"Is that what it does?" he asked on a whisper of laughter. Only she would think of Einstein at a time like this. "You're beautiful. You have a beautiful mind."

"Thank . . . you." Her breath caught, and she gazed at him in a small panic. "Mark," she tried to tell him of the storm that was approaching. Lightning flashed through her.

He took his name from her mouth, covering her lips in an intense kiss of passionate need. She gave in to that need and to her own, and knew the final flash of the storm in a brilliant burst of joy that wrung little whimpering cries from her and brought a groan from her lover as he now pursued his own course in the wildly surging seas of desire.

"Oh, darling, yes, yes," she encouraged, holding him tightly to her as he plunged one last time against her and was still, his breath coming rapidly against her temple.

He kissed her lightly and turned their dampened bodies to rest side by side. Sarah touched the spirals of hair on his chest, splaying her fingers wide over the glistening surface of his skin.

"Are you all right, love?" he asked, a frown on his brow.

"Perfect," she murmured. "Perfectly happy, perfectly content."

"I never meant to be so . . . well, I lost control." He smiled at her, their faces no more than an inch apart as they shared a pillow. "Do you believe now that I want you?"

Later that day, they talked. Holding hands, they walked around the resort village, window-shopping as lovers everywhere did, and exchanged their life stories —the triumphs and disasters of growing up. Each sought insight into the other.

Sarah told Mark the woeful tale of her first love, admitting her age at the time and her zealous integrity. She found she could laugh about it now. With Mark, she knew the difference between real love and a crush.

"I'm glad your experience didn't turn you off men for all time," he commented huskily, giving her a brief hug.

"Me, too. I've grown up a lot since then," she said quietly.

His glance took in her thoughtful poise. She was at her most beautiful at this moment, he realized. A mature woman, somehow older than she had been when this voyage began, but more enticing and more confident in herself as a person. He had given her that. His chest swelled with pride.

"What are you looking so smug about?" she demanded, seeing him straighten his shoulders and lift his chin in the manner of a conquering hero.

"About being your lover," he whispered, planting a kiss on her temple.

She raised one hand to her face, her fist curled under her chin, one finger extended along her cheek in a thinking pose. "Anybody can be great once, but how are you at repeat performances?" Her eyes challenged him, female to male.

"You'll find out," he growled, low-voiced. "Just you wait. Now shall we go change into dinner clothes?" He turned them in the direction of their bungalow.

They ate shrimp sautéed in garlic butter and drank a sparkling white wine that was deliciously dry. They danced long slow dances to hauntingly sad melodies, and Sarah thought her heart would burst with sheer happiness. But beyond the bliss of the evening was the knowledge that tomorrow they would have to go back to the freighter. A brief sorrow moved across her face like a small cloud.

"Don't borrow trouble," Mark said, somehow knowing all her moods and thoughts. His eyes reflected the light of the floating candle on their table.

"It's hard when you can see the end of paradise."

"Yes." A look of anguish darkened his gaze. "Shall we go?"

They drifted down the stairs, their arms wrapped around each other's waists. Stopping on a landing, they watched a sailboat far out on the bay, its white sails taking on a pearly glow in the last sinking rays of sunset. They went to their room.

Mark locked the door behind them, his eyes on Sarah as she turned and faced him. She held out her arms.

This time their coming together was accomplished with the surety of old lovers, each secure with the other. This time neither asked permission from the other to touch; they simply proceeded to help each other undress. Sarah laid the clothes she removed, whether from him or herself, neatly on a chair and received a smile of approval from her lover.

When she climbed into bed, her eyes took on the glow of the evening sun as she waited for him to come to her.

Mark sat beside her for a moment. "When I touch you, I feel as if the gods might strike me down at any moment," he said.

She looked puzzled. "Why?"

"There must be a price for abusing purity," he explained.

Her radiance diminished. She frowned up at him from her position among the pillows. "I'm human, my love." Her tone was slightly chiding. "I'm not as pure or innocent as you seem to think. Don't elevate me to Olympus. I don't belong there. I belong here with you."

Rising to her knees, she laid her hands on his chest. Very slowly she roamed down his hard length, following the contours of his ribs and his abdomen, moving along the grooves of his loins onto his thighs and sweeping back up his lean torso in a caress that was deliberate and provocative.

He caught her hands, brought them to his lips, where he kissed each small palm, then held them against his chest. "And if this is all I can give you? Just this, nothing more?" He indicated their bodies with a movement of his hand.

"I'll take it." She was very sure.

"Oh, love," he said, a thin note of agony in the words. He crushed her lithe softness to him, holding her fiercely, tenderly, while the flames started a dance of fire through their veins.

Sarah let herself be pressed back into the pillows. She felt his kisses falling on her like rain, over her face and her throat and her breasts.

This time, she sensed, their lovemaking was different from what it had been that first time, several hours earlier. That time had been for her; this time was for him.

Her arms held him closer and closer. Her hands searched over him, making sure he knew of his welcome into her embrace. In some way—and she didn't know how she knew this—this loveplay was more than play; it was a benediction, a healing, for him. Whatever he needed from her she wanted to give. She would open herself completely to him.

When he groaned her name with longing, she answered with her own sighing endearments. When he pressed fervent kisses on her breasts, she cradled his head in her arms and whispered of the delight he gave to her. She let him see her pleasure and her need, and he responded to each insight with loving attention.

He brought her ecstasy as if it were an offering to be laid at her feet. He worshiped her body, spoke of her beauty, and let her see the devastating power she had over him. And in the end, she felt as if she were truly the goddess he said she was.

Together they climbed the mountain and together they dwelt at its summit for an endless time, and then they plunged over the edge and floated into tranquillity.

Sarah placed languorous kisses along her lover's throat as she rested against him, her head on his shoulder. "Is it always like this?" she asked in wonder.

"It's the feast of the gods that never loses its flavor," he replied. He shifted their position so he could gaze into her eyes. The glow was still there. "I never realized that something so turbulent could bring such peace in its wake."

A radiant smile bloomed across her face.

His breath caught in his chest as emotion pulsed upward from within. She was so *giving*. Her generosity touched him in places that hadn't been broached in many years. He felt as if he were being opened, cleansed, made whole again.

"Mark," she breathed, inviting him to her.

Very slowly, he made love to her again, watching her face as his passion filled her. He was humbled by what he saw. She was radiant with a luminosity that came from within her, from the fires he fanned into being. To him, she was all the good things that had been missing from his life—the passionate as well as the pure. He felt her tremble, heard her cry, as she reached the crest.

"Thank you," she whispered a minute after that.

He could only recall weeping twice in his life: once when his grandmother had died, and again when he was twenty-one. Now he felt the pressure build behind his eyes. He would never forget this moment, he thought, and the way this woman had responded to him. She acted as if, in giving himself, he had bestowed upon her a gift of priceless treasure, a thing beyond all earthly value; as if, in taking her to heaven, he had given her all her dreams. His arms clasped her in a tender embrace as she settled herself against him and drifted into sleep. He stayed awake, guarding her as if she were his own treasure.

It came to him that men needed their women to be better than they were. They needed them as sources of succor to temper the males' aggressiveness and as ideals of goodness to direct and ennoble the masculine spirit. A man instinctively knew passion, he thought, but he had to learn love. His woman could teach him that.

He tried to reason out why he felt this was so, but he was satiated with their lovemaking and with the simple pleasure of holding her in his arms. She was as soft and light as thistledown, clinging to his side like a small burr. He had to smile at himself. He was getting as sentimental as a poet.

Sarah woke to the strange sensation of being constricted in some manner. She opened her eyes and gazed at her lover.

Mark's arm was across her chest and his leg was thrown over both of hers. His face had been snuggled into her hair, and he wore a look of peace, she noted. She had pleased him and made him happy. It gave her a good feeling to know that. Carefully she began to extricate herself from his hold.

"Where do you think you're going?" he asked without opening his eyes.

She was assailed by an absolutely ridiculous wave of joy. "To the bathroom," she replied saucily, kissing his chin, which was rather scratchy.

He at last freed her, stretching his arms over his head and yawning as she climbed over him. After a while, he rose and joined her in the shower. Much later, he ushered her over to breakfast where he proceeded to eat a huge meal. This drew teasing comments from her about his waistline.

Later they spread their towels over lounge chairs on the beach and soaked up the warm rays of the sun. Half-reclining, Sarah watched the boats on the bay and wished she and Mark could stay in this peaceful place forever. The time for returning was already hanging over her head like the proverbial sword. Only a few hours to go.

"Mark?" she said.

He gave a slight grunt to indicate he was listening.

"You said you were from Indiana. Do you ever go home?" She wanted to ask him about his family, for he had told her nothing of them, other than his grandmother. She sensed a reticence in him to discuss that part of his life.

He sat up, giving her a glance before gazing far out to sea. "No," he stated. His face hardened to forbidding lines, and all at once he seemed different to her, closed and hard.

"Why not? Don't you have any family left there?" she persisted, feeling that there was something in his attitude very basic to understanding him.

He shrugged. "None that I care to see." His face was devoid of emotion.

"Was it so awful, your life back there?" she pried gently.

"Yes. Decadent." He got up from the lounger, and went to stand at the edge of the water.

Sarah followed. "If you want to talk about it, I'll listen," she said, "but if you'd rather not, I'll understand."

His glance cut to her. "Would you?" he asked in a strangely tight voice. "There's not much to tell. It's shocking," he warned.

"That's okay." She steeled herself for whatever he would say. She would show no emotion except possibly sympathy.

"When I graduated from college, I went home that summer and met a girl. We decided to get married." He stopped abruptly as if he hadn't thought of these things in a long while and needed to find the words.

She waited.

"Then one day I found her and my father in the boathouse."

Sarah didn't need to ask what he meant.

"Out of revenge, I decided to seduce my father's mistress." Now he spoke quickly, a cold recitation of facts. "I succeeded—as I was sure I would. I knew a lot about women by then. I had been seduced by one of my mother's friends when I was fifteen."

This statement brought a gasp to Sarah's lips. She barely managed to suppress the shock he had warned her about. "What . . . what happened after that?" she whispered.

"Then I found the mistress's husband in bed with my mother. I was going to kill him until he told me not to be a fool. It seems my parents and he and his wife had been 'friends' for years. I was the only one who didn't know . . . an innocent, you might say." The cynicism had returned to his eyes; there was pain, too.

Sarah wished she had never brought up the subject. It was bad enough about his fiancée, and apparently he had known of his father's mistress, but his mother had occupied a special place in his heart. To the young man, she had been the ideal woman, abused by her husband's lust and infidelity.

Tears filled Sarah's eyes, and she tried to blink them away before he noticed. His hand came up to her face and wiped the moisture from her lashes.

His lips curved into a smile as he gazed down at her.

"It doesn't matter now. I wasn't in love with the girl, only with a romantic dream that existed in my mind." His fingers caressed her cheek. "Except now I'm finding that the dream is a possibility, after all."

She shook her head. "Don't confuse me with a dream. You'll be disappointed." She ached for him, and she thought she understood his feelings toward her, including his worry over her innocence, but she wasn't a saint. Only a genius, she acknowledged with a wry amusement that she hadn't been able to use on herself before now. "So what happened after that? How did you get into . . ." She stopped, not sure she should mention his work.

"I joined the army for four years and was in Intelligence for three of those. When I got out, I started working for the Company. I was in London for a year, then assigned to Paris, which is still my home base, although I've traveled throughout the Middle East and Europe for several years now." He cited only the main facts of his life.

Sarah refrained from asking him about the widow. Perhaps it was better not to know. "Race you to that rock," she said, diving into the clear blue water.

And so they played in the water until it was time for lunch. After that, they prepared to leave. As Mark drove down the twisting drive along the cliff, Sarah refused to glance over her shoulder. She wouldn't look back, not once, not ever . . . for each time she did, she felt as if they were being cast out of Eden.

9

The freighter was in port when they arrived back in Hērákleion in the middle of the afternoon. Baruch stood on deck in a seaman's stance with his legs braced against the roll of the ship, his face an unrevealing mask as usual. Everyone else greeted the errant couple as if they were prodigal children.

Later as the freighter moved off down the coast Sarah studied the land from her favorite perch on the railing. Rows of olive trees gleamed gray-green in the lengthening rays of sunlight. Grapevines twined along fences around every vegetable garden while nut and citrus groves undulated over the foothills. Behind it all, the mountains, snowcapped and beautiful, rose to soaring heights.

"This is a lovely place. I'll always remember it," she said to Mark. Her eyes became shadowed.

He lifted her hand and placed it on his thigh, keeping his hand over hers. "Don't start looking ahead yet. We have another week left." But his voice, when he spoke, was deeper, and his face was pensive after that.

After picking up a load of raisins at a small port, the freighter moved on out to sea, heading for Rhodes, the isle of roses. As evening advanced the surface of the water reflected the fiery pinks and golds of the sky until the whole world seemed bathed in gorgeous color.

"Beautiful, isn't it?" Mark offered. "It's easy to see why the old gods loved Greece. I can almost imagine them here, strolling on the beaches of the islands, talking, laughing . . . loving." He said the last word very softly, bending over her as he did.

Sarah pointed toward the sunset. "In geometry, there's a point called the *point of infinity* where all parallel lines come together. Maybe the gods live there now."

Wrapping his arms around her, Mark folded her against his chest, his lips nuzzling the curls along her temple. Silently they watched the panorama until twilight claimed the heavens.

The evening meal was pleasant, and the conversation centered on Rhodes, their last stop before returning to Mykonos and then Piraiévs. The passengers planned to catch airplanes from Athens to their respective homes. Captain Theodopoulos and the crew would begin their circuitous route all over again.

There was something very likable about Michael Renfro, Sarah decided as, after dinner at the Englishman's hotel, they all went for a walk along the busy street. She and Mark, after a long night and day at sea, had gone to meet Michael as soon as the ship had arrived at the port at Rhodes. The day was Thursday. In six days, they were due in Piraiévs.

"Nothing new has turned up," Michael said, concluding his report to Mark as they strolled along. "By the way," he mentioned in an offhand manner to Sarah, "it's a pleasure to know the person responsible for completing Project 992."

Sarah couldn't prevent the startled jerk of her eyes to his. Then she looked away, her expression closed. Baruch . . . Achinson . . . had known of her involvement with that code-breaking project, too. He had tried to probe her for information about it last night when he, Mark, and she had talked on deck after dinner, but then, as now, she said nothing. She never discussed anything that went on in her office outside the building. That way, she didn't have to worry about a slip of the tongue.

Michael changed the subject, and they talked of trivial matters. Stopping at a taverna, they went in and took a table, the men ordering beer and Sarah sticking to a bottled, flavored mineral water.

"I read that Edgar Allan Poe was a cryptanalyst of renown. Is that true?" Michael asked.

Sarah studied him for a moment before answering. Although he was lounging back in his chair in a lazy pose, she noticed the same alert wariness about him that Mark had. And Baruch, too. Finally she nodded. "He showed that, in a message of reasonable length, no simple substitution cipher resisted solution."

"I had a secret code ring when I was a kid. My friends and I loved to send secret messages to one another that our parents couldn't read." Michael chuckled. "How long have people been fascinated by things like that, I wonder?"

"The earliest known cryptograms were sent by the Spartans around 400 B.C.," Sarah told him, warming to the subject. "It was the style then to wear ribbon bands with abstract designs and lettering on them. So the military leaders sent ciphered messages by wrapping a piece of ribbon around a cylinder, writing the instructions for battle on the cloth, then giving the ribbon to a courier who would wear it around his head or waist until he reached the battle commander. Then the ribbon would be wrapped around a cylinder of the same size as the original and read. Pretty smart, huh?"

The two men looked impressed. Mark was mostly silent while Michael and Sarah continued their discussion.

"So there're only three basic ways of encrypting information," she concluded her lecture enthusiastically. "Coding, which uses a secret language; ciphering, which uses substitution and transposition of letters to hide the message; and concealment—that's invisible inks and such."

Michael suddenly looked stern. "You have given yourself away entirely."

"What?" she said, not understanding. She glanced at Mark, but his expression told her nothing. "What do you mean?" she demanded of Michael.

He counted off the items on his fingers. "I have learned the following facts in the last hour. You are an expert at cryptology. . . ."

"But you already knew that," she protested defensively.

"Also, the types of analysis you use include the Kasiski and 'probable word' methods and the Kerckhoffs technique for extraction of key words used in ciphering. All facts I didn't know before our discussion."

Sarah shrugged. "And all facts which can be found in any elementary text on cryptology."

"That's not the point. If you were questioned by an interrogator skilled in math, how much more would he be able to draw out of you without your realizing it?" He turned to Mark. "I think that's why no one has attacked you and Achinson directly. They want her alive, and they can't take a chance that she might get killed by a stray bullet in a shoot-out. They need to find out about the intercepted coded tape and how close she is to solving it." His gaze went to Sarah. "A mind like that in the wrong hands . . ."

Michael's words brought home to Mark just how important, how brilliant Sarah was. He had been seeing her as a young, inexperienced woman, although he knew she was considered a genius of the first order. He was a fool, and he had made the worst mistake an agent could make. He had gotten emotionally involved, seeing Sarah as he wanted to see her, not as she really was. But it was too late for recriminations, he thought wearily.

Sarah was jolted back into the world of reality. How many people knew of the satellite transmission that had been tape-recorded and brought to her for solution? How many knew that it had contained information on a satellite weapons system that had been banned by international agreement and that she had broken the code of the transmission? She sighed, feeling the burden of her knowledge like a weight on her shoulders. And she was a danger to these men, she realized.

"I suppose I should go home," she said slowly. "I'm just a problem to everyone."

Michael shook his head. "I don't think there's any need to worry now that we have those two 'burglars' locked up." He grinned at the couple. "Have fun tomorrow, and I'll see you here tomorrow night. Around nine?" he asked, verifying the time.

They agreed and returned to the freighter while Michael went back to his hotel. Mark told Achinson of their sight-seeing plans for the next day before joining Sarah in her cabin.

It was two o'clock by the time Mark and Sarah began their trip to the seacoast village of Líndos. They had toured the walled city built by the Knights Hospitalers of Saint John of Jerusalem, who were now called the Knights of Malta, all that morning.

Memories of last night in Mark's arms brought an instant rush of warmth to Sarah's whole body. His lips on hers, his touch, so careful and tender, had excited her beyond her ability to think or reason. There had only been sensation . . . and the great love she felt for him. His words to her had been sweet and teasing.

"The spy who came in from the cold," he had said as they lay in an intimate embrace.

"And how is it?" she had asked.

"Nice," he'd said. He'd tilted his head to one side and kissed her. "Very nice." He'd tilted his head to the other side and kissed her again. "So very, very nice."

She had sighed, feeling happiness and sadness all mixed together inside her.

"Each time with you is different, like starting anew." He had gazed down at her, a message just for her on his face.

Grief, she thought now as they rode along the winding seacoast road. A parting. A good-bye. That was what he had been telling her.

Lindos sat on a short peninsula on the southeastern side of the island, an hour's drive from the capital. Nestled in an old ravine, it was quaint in the manner loved by artists.

Mark and Sarah arrived and, taking their picnic lunch, started on a hike up to the top of the cliff. As they puffed their way up the mile-long footpath, they met several groups of tourists who were already making a descent.

"Oh, this is marvelous," Sarah exclaimed when they reached the summit. The view was inspiring—sapphire water; whitewashed houses tucked into the ravine; a fortress and an acropolis, which they explored thoroughly; and a flower-covered slope falling away from the stone walls.

"Shall we eat here?" She indicated some convenient rocks in the field of daisies and wild poppies.

A young couple with three children were trailing around the ruins.

"Let's see if we can't find a better spot," Mark suggested. Taking her hand, he led her along a path until they came to a small clearing. To their left, a narrow gully filled with low-growing shrubs dipped toward the sea. Trees lined its perimeter and circled behind them, forming a natural screen. The land rose slightly into a hillock to their right while the view in front was open to the sea.

"It's almost six," Sarah noted.

"We'll have to eat and start back." Mark reminded her of the passage of time.

They ate silently while the sun dropped into the curved bowl of the sea. Each moment formed a separate memory and a separate pain in her heart.

"Sarah, when we get back . . ." Mark began.

"Don't," she pleaded. "I don't want to talk about it."

"We have to."

"Not today," she insisted.

"All right," he conceded.

She got up and drifted about, looking at the stones that littered the area, then admiring a group of small flowers. Finally Mark rose and repacked the carryall, slinging the strap over his shoulder. It was time to go.

Just as he was about to speak, a sound like an angry hornet buzzed near his ear. He didn't see anything. He bent over to pick up a scrap of paper, and in that instant, he heard another wasp whiz by. Realization struck him like lightning.

"Sarah, get down!"

Just as Mark shouted at her, Sarah felt an incredible pain in her arm. She looked at it, seeing her blouse sleeve strangely torn and her arm suddenly wounded.

Mark dived for her, taking her down to the ground and rolling them behind a low outcropping of rock and bushes.

"My arm," she said, holding it against her body.

"You've been shot," he explained tersely. "Shhh," he cautioned. He raised his head, listening intently. Judging from where he had been standing and from Sarah's position when she had been hit, their gunman had to be behind the rocky point of the hill. Were there more than one?

The noisy family with the children had evidently finished their sightseeing; they were following a nearby path back down the cliff. If Sarah and Mark could join them, they would have a chance. Mark was sure the man hadn't meant to hurt Sarah. That third shot had been fired off hastily, to try and prevent Mark from reaching her.

"Come on," he ordered. "Keep low. Try not to make any noise."

Bent almost to the ground, they kept the rocks between them and their attacker until they reached the shrubs along the gully. Slipping past those, they made it to the trees. Above them, the family continued their descent, stopping now and then to admire some new sight, and once, to tie a shoelace.

Through a haze of burning pain, Sarah heard the

mother fussing at one of the children about his shoe-laces being undone. Holding her arm, she blindly followed Mark and did what he told her.

Mark urged Sarah out into the path. This way the family acted as a shield between them and the man taking the potshots at him. He experienced a stab of conscience. Was he putting those people in danger? His first thought had been for Sarah, but now he had to consider others as they approached the small town.

Glancing over his shoulder, he saw no one. They seemed safe for the moment. He hurried Sarah along faster. Just as the path widened at the end, a familiar figure pounded toward them.

Baruch, breathless, ran to them. "I've been trying to find you. There's trouble." He noticed Sarah. "What happened?"

"She's been shot. It's just a flesh wound. Have you got a handkerchief?"

Baruch handed over the bandana from around his neck, and Mark quickly bound it around Sarah's arm. There wasn't much blood, but it ached fiercely, as if hot needles were being driven into her skin. She felt hurt over Mark's light dismissal of her injury. He finished the task, and they both turned back to Baruch, who now held a gun in his hand—pointed directly at them.

Mark took a step forward, putting himself in front of Sarah.

"You're not faster than a speeding bullet," Baruch warned him, waving the gun slightly. "Go in front. The girl and I will follow. Don't try anything. I'd hate for her to get hurt in a scuffle."

Mark started down the short road into town with Sarah behind him and Baruch following. "Where to?" he asked, his voice devoid of expression.

"Your car will do for now. I'll see that it's returned to the rental agency tomorrow with apologies for being a day late."

Mark led the way to the town square, where the car was parked. So they only had one day. Tomorrow Sarah would be taken off the island. How? Airplane? Ship? He had no illusions about what his fate would be. He would be dead. A message would be delivered to the freighter saying that the two of them had decided to fly back to Athens; thus Captain Theodopoulos would have no need to worry about their safety. That left Michael Renfro.

"You'll drive," Baruch said to Mark. "She and I will ride in the back. We'll have another passenger."

They climbed into the auto and waited. A few minutes later, another man emerged from the path, jumped into the front seat beside Mark, and turned to smile at Sarah.

She recoiled from his pleasant greeting and his apology for her wound. Close up, the man's gap-toothed smile and tobacco odor were distinctly recognizable—the cigarette-smoking man on the Delos trip. So many levels of betrayal, she thought.

Baruch told Mark to start the car and gave him directions to follow, then he harshly reprimanded his accomplice for his clumsiness in missing Mark and hitting Sarah. The man gave Sarah another smile, this one apologetic.

Not long after the journey started, Baruch directed Mark to turn onto a road that was no more than two ruts through a tree-lined meadow. They slowed to a crawl. Finally they reached a small house built into the side of a hill. Another building, a stout shed, stood a few yards from it.

A shepherd's home, Sarah realized. It looked abandoned, but there was still a strong animal scent in the air. Baruch motioned Mark into the interior of the shed. He snapped a padlock into place after the door was closed.

At the cottage, Sarah was taken inside and handcuffed to the end of a cot. Baruch spoke to the other man, calling him Jori. They spoke sometimes in English, but most of their conversation was in Greek. She felt an acute sense of helplessness. Mark would die because of her.

She lay down, but rest was far from her mind. Her eyes searched the cottage, but there was no chance for escape. The two men slept fitfully in chairs all night. At one point, Jori brought a jacket and placed it over her. She closed her eyes, not wanting to look at either of her abductors. He touched her forehead, then spoke to Baruch.

"A fever," the older man said and shrugged. "It isn't uncommon with a flesh wound."

Jori took a bucket and went out. When he came back, he gave Sarah a drink of water. It was dark outside, she noted. She must have slept some.

The morning sky was bright with dawn when she woke again. A knock at the door woke the two men, and Baruch unbolted the wooden panel cautiously. Two strangers came in, and their entrance brought smiles to her captors' faces. They all exchanged greetings and conversed in low tones.

Sarah experienced a despair as deep as a bottomless pit. They would never escape now. She watched through barely opened eyes as Jori spoke, glancing worriedly at her. One of the newcomers talked in reassuring tones, and they prepared to leave.

Sarah's hand was freed, and she was pulled to her feet. Baruch checked her temperature with a hand on her face. Jori brought her another drink before they started out.

Once outside they turned toward the shed. Sarah tried to think of something to do. "If you hurt him, I'll never cooperate," she warned Baruch. "You'll have to drag me, kicking and screaming."

He grinned, shook his head, and unlocked the door. The shed was empty. Sarah's eyes widened. There was a hurried muttered conference. Turning, Jori led the way down a steep path toward a small cove, where a motor launch was pulled up on a strip of beach. Farther out to sea, she could see a larger vessel.

She felt detached from everything, as if only her body were with the men. Her real self watched all this from a distance. She wondered where Mark was. *Please, let him be safe.*

At the end of the path, Baruch fell back, staying in a group of trees while the others dashed ahead to the boat. But before they reached it, other figures were suddenly present. Noise and confusion and shouts were heard all along the cove.

With a muffled curse, Baruch pulled Sarah back along the path up the cliff, but he veered off course before they reached the cottage. He was circling the area, she realized, probably to see if he could get to the car without being spotted.

Silence sat like a shroud on the two tiny buildings. Not a bird called; not a cricket sang. Not even the drone of a bee broke the quiet of the place. The hair stood up on Sarah's neck.

Baruch's hand clamped around her mouth and she was pulled farther into the woods. When they were far enough away, he released her. He pointed the gun directly at her. "You are nothing to me now. But you do mean something to *them*. Walk," he ordered, motioning in the direction he wanted her to go.

As they started off a noise brought their eyes around to the trees behind them. Nothing. Baruch grabbed Sarah, holding her in front of him as a shield. "Come on out, or I'll kill her." He pressed the gun barrel against her temple.

Slowly Mark walked out into the open. His eyes flicked over Sarah and then to Baruch. "You'll never make it," he advised coolly.

"Neither will she." His voice was evil. "Should you have sharpshooters in the woods, the shot that kills me will trigger the one that kills her."

"No sharpshooters," Mark denied. "This is just between you and me. Let her go and face me like a man."

Baruch's hold tightened around Sarah's waist. She drew a loud breath, then let it out in a low moan. Her body slumped into a faint, her weight going dead on his arm. He stooped as she slowly sank toward the ground, keeping her between him and the man whose expression never changed as the gun was lifted toward him.

Sarah's teeth clamped into Baruch's leg, biting in past the denim of his pants and breaking the skin. She bit as hard as she possibly could and heard his shout of pain. Then she was bowled over as Mark knocked her captor backward.

Mark's hand closed on the gun and he rolled and stood, giving the gun a mighty toss that carried it out of sight into the bushes. "Move, Sarah," he barked and she did, running for safety behind the nearest tree. Mark's eyes narrowed on his enemy. "Now," he said, and the word brought a shiver to Sarah's nerves.

But Baruch wasn't through. With a deft movement, he pulled his knife, the blade flicking out with a deadly gleam as he pressed the release button. "She's not worth dying for," he advised Mark.

"I'm not going to die," Mark said, a wolfish smile

appearing briefly on his intent face. The two men circled the small clearing, measuring each other.

"It was a shame to waste that brain on a female," Baruch commented.

"Jealous?" Mark taunted.

"I could have done more with it," Baruch bragged. He rushed suddenly, closing in with perilous speed. He lashed out with his right hand, but Mark sidestepped quickly. "I should have taken care of you years ago," he said. His knife flashed. "I sent a boy to do a man's job, but now, I'll handle you myself." His laugh was confident.

"So you were behind the Paris attempt," Mark mused. "Renfro told me that you were the agent on the missing diplomat case, too."

"Yes. A successful mission," the double agent admitted. He feinted to the right, switched hands on the knife, and dove toward Mark's unprotected abdomen.

The young man was quicker. He leapt back, sucking in his belly, and felt the stir of air as the blade passed him. His shirt had been slashed. A close call.

His mind seemed to click into some primitive mode of survival that sharpened his senses and produced a cunning he hadn't known he possessed. He moved forward, forcing Baruch back. The other man crouched and sprang, switching the blade back to his right hand.

Mark got his left arm up in time to block the stabbing blow. He waded in with a right smash to the ribs, feeling the give of bone and flesh under his knuckles. There was a satisfying *whuff* of expelled air as Baruch moved to the side, out of range. Now Mark was the aggressor, moving in, pushing Baruch from side to side in the narrow space.

Baruch bent, lashed upward with the knife, and then, while Mark was busy avoiding the blade, drove an uppercut to his middle. Mark managed to tense his stomach muscles before the blow could stun his diaphragm. He landed a cuff on Baruch's ear that wasn't very effective, then drove a knee into his opponent's chest, but they were too close, and the blow was too short to stop the man.

Baruch grabbed Mark's leg and, with a sideways twist, forced him off balance. Realizing that he was falling, Mark gripped Baruch's wrist, keeping the knife-wielding hand away from his face and throat. With his free hand, he hooked the other man's shoulders and jerked, pulling them both down. Now both men wrestled for the advantage as they struggled in the dust and grass.

Sarah watched in horrified fascination as they fought. They were equally matched. Mark's reflexes and slightly greater strength were offset by Baruch's weapon and greater experience. The sounds of their thrashing bodies and gasping breaths were the only noises in the forest as the life-and-death battle went on.

It was a clash of Titans, of good against evil. They engaged, struck, parried, and fell back, both men now bleeding and bruised. Mark had a knife cut along his ribs; Baruch bled from a blow above one eye. Both men had bloody noses.

A surprise kick when he had been expecting the flick of the knife doubled Mark over as pain lanced through him from cracked ribs. Baruch leapt to the offense, clubbing downward with his fist. Mark rolled and managed to fend off the attack once more. With a karate chop to the wrist, he dislodged the knife, sending it flying a safe distance away.

"Now," he gritted. No longer fearing the lethal steel, he pressed forward with both fists, striking again and again in upward blows that drove the other man off.

Then they were standing, slugging it out, and the younger man's determination overcame the other's desperation as Baruch realized he was no match for the fury that filled his enemy.

With a final right to the chin from Mark, Baruch sank to his knees. "Stand up," Mark ordered, pulling him to his feet, then hitting him again. And again. And again.

A hand touched Sarah's arm. She whirled around to stare at Michael Renfro.

"Go to him. Stop him," Michael said. "You can do it with a word. I would have to use force." He gave her a little push.

She crossed the trampled arena and touched Mark's arm as he hauled Baruch to his feet yet another time. "Mark, don't. No more."

His eyes flicked to her and slowly they cleared of the blood-rage that filled him. "Sarah," he said and caught her to him, burying his face in the soft sweetness of her neck, holding her tightly as if she were his only path back to sanity.

"I have a plane on standby in Rhodes," Michael mentioned as he snapped handcuffs on Baruch and lifted him to his feet. "Would you like a lift over to Athens?" he inquired in his customary understated manner.

The next few hours passed in a daze for Sarah as Michael drove the rental car back to the city of Rhodes. She sat in the front between him and Mark.

"What will happen to them?" she asked. "Baruch, I mean, Achinson, and Jori and the other two."

"I'm not positive, but I think they will be extradited to the States for trial," Mark said. "Or they'll face charges of kidnapping and attempted murder under Greek law."

"Was anyone on the beach hurt?" she asked.

"One of their men was wounded; one of ours turned his ankle on a rock," Michael answered, chuckling. "Clumsy fellow."

"How did you get out of the shed?" She spoke to Mark.

He raised his hands, showing her the splinter marks in his fingers. "I pried a board off last night."

"People were injured because of my foolishness," she said. Her eyes were shadowed with regret.

"No more than they deserved," Michael told her. "And we might never have caught on to Achinson if it hadn't been for you." Then to Mark: "Sorry I didn't tell you sooner that he was the one who worked with me on the missing diplomat case. I had to be sure of your loyalties."

Mark indicated that he understood, and they lapsed into silence.

"The world of intrigue," Sarah muttered. "It seems a terribly hard life."

"Sometimes it is," Michael agreed.

She glanced at Mark, but he said nothing.

By midafternoon, Sarah was installed in a hotel suite in Athens. A doctor had been summoned, and he had given her a shot of penicillin and some tablets for pain. He cleaned and bandaged her arm. Marine guards from the embassy were posted at her door.

"A classic example of closing the barn door after the horse gets out, wouldn't you say?" Michael grinned at Mark, who nodded agreement.

Sarah improved steadily during the next week. On Thursday, the doctor pronounced her well enough to go home. Her temperature had been normal for two days, and her arm was healing without complications.

Michael and Mark had been in to see her several

times each day, although they were obviously busy with their "case," as they called it.

"Damnation," Michael exclaimed on Thursday evening when he dropped by. "These international cases are so full of red tape."

Sarah sympathized with him over all the paperwork he had to fill out. She knew Mark was even busier. When he came in an hour later, Michael said good-bye and left. There was a brief intense silence after his departure.

"You'll have a scar," Mark said finally.

"A souvenir of my vacation," she replied, smiling. Then she saw the look in his eyes. She went to him and laid her hand on his arm. "It doesn't matter. It's only a scar. It doesn't hurt anymore."

His hands lifted to her shoulders, and his fingers massaged her gently through the blouse she wore. Their clothes had been flown up to them, along with best wishes from the freighter's crew and passengers. "How do you feel? Are you well enough to travel?" he asked.

She had been hoping for more, she realized, but his words weren't unexpected. She had prepared herself for the parting. "Of course." Her voice sounded kind. She was trying to make it easy for him.

"Your plane reservation is tomorrow," he said in the softest tones possible, as if to lessen the blow.

"All right."

"You won't see them or know who they are, but there'll be people around you, watching after you. You don't have to be afraid that anyone will hurt you." He lowered his hands and walked away from her. "I'll be going to Paris for a short period, maybe a month, to tie up loose ends and file my report on Achinson."

"I see." She sat in a velvet chair and waited.

"We'll have to figure out how much harm he might have caused on other cases he was involved in and check to see if . . . well, never mind. Anyway, he will be brought home and tried for treason." Mark moved restlessly around the room.

Sarah knew that he was searching for a way to say good-bye without hurting her feelings, and her heart ached for him. She tried to think of a way to say it for him. "Well," she started.

"I'll come to you, but first I have these things I have to do," he interrupted, speaking hastily, needing to get the words out.

"I know. I understand," she said, not sure that she did. Would he really come to her? When? For how long?

He came over and sat on the arm of her chair. He smoothed the hair at her temple, running his fingers through the curls again and again. "Christmas curls," he said and smiled at her.

They talked until her bedtime, and then he kissed her once before he left.

The next afternoon Michael accompanied Mark and Sarah to the airport. When it was time for her to board the plane, he kissed her once on each cheek. "I have a daughter. Her mother and I were divorced when she was young, so I never knew her very well. She's married now and lives in Canada."

Sarah waited while he chose his words, a task that appeared difficult for him. "I'm sorry," she said in the long pause.

His smile was sad. "I hope she's like you," he finished.

"I don't need a father, Michael, but if you'd like, I'll be your friend."

"Done, then," he said, and they shook on it.

She turned to Mark. He bent to her and kissed her briefly. A kiss to last a lifetime, she thought, but she managed a smile. "Thank you for watching out for me."

"I'll see you," he said. His eyes were like a winter storm as he watched her until she disappeared inside the plane.

Sarah peered out the window and waited for the flight back to the States to begin. A long journey home, she thought. Her fingers found the gold chain and followed it to the pelican hidden beneath her blouse. "Good-bye, my love," she whispered as the force of the takeoff pushed her into her seat. "May the gods forever smile on you."

10

On the long flight back to the States, Sarah slept fitfully, often waking with a frantic jump of every nerve in her body. She missed the comfort of Mark's arms and wondered if she would ever know that heaven again. She didn't think so.

He had lived a life of adventure and intrigue too long to settle down to her restricted existence. Who could blame him? Her own glimpse of freedom had opened a vista to her spirit that would never be completely closed. She had gazed upon distant times and misty dreams, and she would never forget them. They were locked forever in her heart.

Dr. Fielding met her at the airport and accompanied her to her apartment, which was only a Metro-stop from the Pentagon. He carefully probed into her psyche for the next two days, and she, just as carefully, rebuffed him.

"So how do you feel about the outcome of your

vacation?" he asked after dinner that first night. "Did it live up to your expectations?"

"Yes, it did," she said, smiling at the understatement in her answer. With a talent for evasion that she hadn't known she possessed, she told him enough to satisfy his professional worries but no more.

"I knew, of course, as soon as they told me you had gone to Greece, why you had chosen that country," he said wisely. "It's your intellectual home."

She smiled at him affectionately. "And now I'm glad to be really home."

He nodded slowly, mulling her words over, seeking their deeper meaning. "Yes," he said at last, "home is where the heart is."

"Would you like more coffee?" she asked him.

Her heart wasn't here, she thought. It was out someplace roaming the world. Home, she decided, was where you went when you couldn't follow your heart. This was where she would wait for Mark even if he never came to her. Acknowledging that a person could become used to a way of life and be unable, or unwilling, to change, she knew she would accept any bits of himself that he wanted to give her. Perhaps he would come visit her when he was in the States.

The next afternoon she went to the airport with Dr. Fielding. He had assured her and her boss that she had come through her ordeal with flying colors. Sarah gravely thanked him for coming in person to check on her mental health. On the way back to her apartment, she realized that she had outgrown her mentor. She was no longer willing to share her deepest thoughts with him, nor her strongest emotions. Only one person in the world had total access to her.

* * *

The rain was dreary, blowing in sheets across the streets of Paris. Mark studied the leaden sky as he ate his midafternoon lunch without much interest.

"I say," a voice spoke near him, "do you know the quickest way to get to Athens?"

A smile spread across the younger man's face as he stood and stretched out a hand. "Michael! Where the heck have you been this past month?" he demanded good-naturedly.

"In the States," Michael informed him. He hung up his tweed overcoat after shaking the moisture from it.

The smile left the clean-cut features. "How is she?"

"Fine. Lonely, I'd say. Missing you like hell but not showing it. She's brave, you know." Michael pulled out a chair and settled himself wearily in it. He had been traveling a great deal during the past four weeks, first to Canada to see his daughter, and then to the States to check on Sarah.

Mark continued his perusal of the outdoors, but he wasn't really looking at the rain. Instead, he was seeing a sun-filled beach, a gilded sky, and a warm, sweet woman who smiled up at him from the golden sand with love and trust shining from her eyes, warming him clear through.

"You could write," Michael suggested.

Mark shook his head. "It wouldn't be fair."

"Fair?"

The slate-colored eyes deepened with thoughts he had shared with no one else, but, of course, Michael was special. He had been the means of rescuing Sarah. "By the way, thanks for bringing in the cavalry. How did you know we needed you?"

"You were supposed to meet me at nine. When you didn't show up, I started making inquiries. When I discovered that Achinson was also missing, I went into action and rounded up the Greek police plus a couple of friends of mine who were in the area." He grinned. "I say, I rather liked being a hero and riding to the rescue and all that. Maybe I'll be knighted."

Mark had to laugh.

"When are you going to do something about Sarah?" Michael demanded, getting back to his main concern.

"I'll be leaving here in a couple of days. I've resigned my position and have been tying up loose ends, getting everything out of the way before I leave." His face clouded with worry. "I had to do it this way. I had to give her time, away from me and away from danger, to sort out her feelings. I wanted to be fair to her. Now I'm afraid she might not, well . . . being back home with her friends and all . . ."

Michael was sympathetic. "I don't think you have any worries on that score."

Mark was silent. It had been a long time since he had been unsure of himself, especially with the opposite sex. But what if Sarah didn't want him? What if, to her, their affair had been only a vacation fling? She had had her adventure, and now she was home. Did she need him in her life?

Michael ordered a cup of tea and stared out the window with a sour look on his face. Mark smiled at the disgruntled expression. Everyone was on Sarah's side, he thought, including his boss, who wanted him to stay on the job, hinting that accommodation for a brilliant wife could be made within the Company. But Mark wanted Sarah to see him in ordinary circumstances.

He would court her, he decided. He would take it easy with her, let her get to know him. They could go places, movies and the theater, all those things that women liked to do. Hell, he'd even study math and read up on cryptography if she wanted him to. Then, when she knew him as a person, really knew him, then he would ask her to marry him.

He wouldn't make love to her or use passion to persuade her during that time, he vowed. His intentions would be perfectly straightforward and honorable.

Just for a minute, he spared a thought for Daniel. What if she were seeing the other man? What if more than friendship had grown up between the two of them?

Michael took a sip of tea and put down the cup. "I'll be in Canada for Christmas. I thought I would pop on down and visit you two after the holidays, if you don't mind?"

Mark nodded as his friend took it for granted that he and Sarah would be together. Two more days and he would find out.

"I should get my body in gear and go home," Jennifer said for the third time. She was slumped down on the sofa in Sarah's apartment, her feet propped on the coffee table.

Sarah glanced up from her needlepoint. She now had four of the chair cushions finished and was working on the fifth. "Are you sure it's okay for you to drive?"

"Yeah. I'll beat the five o'clock traffic," Jennifer assured her friend. Then: "Aren't you ever going to tell me about the man you met?" She smoothed the material of her skirt over her flat abdomen, which showed no sign that she was two months pregnant.

"How did you know there was a man?" Sarah asked curiously.

"Sometimes you stare off into space," Jenn explained as if that made total sense.

To Sarah, it did. "Well," she began on a sigh, "he was wonderful, brave, and kind." That she had used the past tense was not lost on either of them.

"Don't you think he will ever come here? Maybe visit you one day?" Jenn asked kindly.

The expression in the brown eyes was opaque, although Sarah's smile was gentle. "I don't think so. Would you like another glass of iced tea?"

The change in subject effectively closed the topic to discussion. There were some things, Sarah thought, that she just couldn't share with anyone, not even with Jennifer. Her memories of Mark were in that group.

"Whatever your vacation did for you, it did wonders for me," Jenn commented with a little laugh. "I think it got all my body parts to working right, being so scared when those men came around and started questioning me on your whereabouts. Tom got mad and threatened to slug one of them if he didn't leave me alone. I think that kind of turned him on, getting to act the hero. The next thing we knew I was pregnant again!"

They laughed together in understanding, two women who each loved a man.

"Well, I really have to get going. My in-laws are coming over to dinner tonight to celebrate the conception." She lifted her eyes heavenward, then grinned as she got up and slipped into her shoes. "Sure you won't come over and join us?"

Sarah helped Jennifer gather her things. "No, thanks. I've got chores to do here." Chatting, she went to the elevator with her friend and said a final good-bye before returning to her apartment and closing the door behind her. It was Saturday, July 28th, she realized, looking at the decorative calendar on her kitchen wall while she placed their glasses in the dishwasher.

It had been six weeks since she had left Greece. Two

more weeks and Daniel would call for the dinner date. He had sent her a note that simply read: THINKING OF YOU, DANIEL. He was nice. Maybe she would accept the invitation, after all.

Picking up a pair of earrings she had left on the windowsill, she returned them to the jewelry box in her bedroom. After putting them into the box, she lingered for a minute, gazing at the necklace that gleamed against the blue velvet lining. With a caressing motion, she touched the pelican and remembered what it had been like to be young and in love and on vacation in paradise. That seemed a hundred years ago.

Studying her face in the mirror, she tried to decide if she looked different, but she couldn't recall how she had looked before she went to Greece. It was just as well that the outside changes took place at a slower rate than the internal ones, she mused.

Going to her desk in a corner of the living room, she began work on a random number generator she was developing for use in a computer application, part of her latest assignment. Her mind wasn't on the task, though. She tossed the pencil aside and paced about the attractive room, her eyes glancing over the impulsively bought items that resided on the mantel or on the polished surfaces of the end tables.

Why did she feel so restless?

Her eyes swept the area, stopping on her needlepoint. She picked up the material, glared at it, then stuffed it back into her sewing basket, and put the whole project out of sight under the end table next to the wall. She was tired of working on that.

The doorbell rang, and she went into the entrance hall with its marble floor and hanging plants that gave it an aura of seclusion like a hidden glen. What had Jenn forgotten?

178

She flicked the button and the small screen in the wall niche came to life, showing her the visitor's face.

Her lips parted on a gasp that didn't get past her throat. Slate gray eyes seemed to be staring at her as Mark looked directly into the hidden camera, knowing it was there. He smiled in a slightly lopsided way that caused her heart to miss several beats, then flutter like mad. She pushed the release that signaled to the doorman that it was okay to let him come up.

While she waited she tried to compose herself. He was probably just passing through this way and had stopped by to say hello. That was all this visit meant. Otherwise why hadn't he contacted her during all this time? Not one call! Not one note!

She would be poised, she decided, so that he wouldn't know what his presence did to her. She would say, "Mark, how lovely to see you again!" when she opened the door. Her voice would contain just the right amount of warm surprise, indicating her pleasure at seeing an old friend.

It was a good thing she had cleaned house and gone grocery-shopping that morning. Maybe he would stay for dinner. She would grill a steak. And they could have cake for dessert. And frozen strawberries. She could thaw them in the microwave oven. Her mind ran feverishly in several directions, then went blank as the buzzer sounded at her door.

She stood rooted to the spot, and for a second, she didn't think she could move a muscle, but finally she did. Taking a deep breath, she opened the door.

Mark stood there, his suitcoat slung over his shoulder, his tie off, and his shirt unbuttoned at the neck. "Hello, young Sarah," he said.

She threw herself into his arms.

179

All his honorable intentions vanished, and he held her crushed to him, ignoring the pain the embrace caused his tender ribs, feeling only the sense of belonging that came to him directly from her.

"Mark, oh, Mark," she babbled incoherently. "I didn't think you would ever come. Oh, Mark!"

He laughed, a man's uninhibited sound of happiness. "Let's go inside," he suggested, turning her with an arm around her shoulders and guiding them past the threshold.

"Oh, yes." She was at once the concerned hostess. "Let me take your coat." She took it and hung it in the closet. "Come in. Would you like some coffee? Are you hungry? I have some cake. There're strawberries in the freezer."

She stopped talking and looked at him, noting how handsome he was in the light blue dress shirt that did wonderful things to his eyes, turning them silvery blue. His dark slacks molded the lean power of his hips and thighs with faithful accuracy. His hair was freshly cut, shorter than it had been in Greece.

"I am hungry," he admitted.

"I have some steaks. We can grill them. I can bake potatoes in the microwave. A salad . . ."

"Just something quick," he said. "An omelet would do."

"I have lots of eggs," she said as if it were a most serious matter. She led him into the kitchen, and he sat at the breakfast bar while she prepared the meal. It pleased him that she was nervous and flustered as she beat eggs and got out bread for toast. She put on a pot of coffee, her hands shaking slightly.

He had been tense the whole way here from Paris,

he realized. Watching her now, he knew her feelings hadn't changed. She was unable to conceal her agitation around him. He smiled and relaxed. Maybe she could summon up subterfuge around others, but not around him.

"How have you been?" she asked breathlessly.

"Fine. My ribs are still a little sore," he confessed.

"From where Baruch . . . Achinson . . . kicked you?"

"Yes."

Her mouth compressed into a thin line, and she looked fierce as she glanced at his face. There was a small scar at the corner of his mouth. She removed a plate from the cupboard and flipped his omelet onto it. After buttering toast, she set the meal in front of him, remembering to give him silverware and a napkin. She poured them each a cup of coffee and joined him at the bar.

"Have you seen Michael Renfro? He stopped by to see me a few days ago on his way back to Europe."

Mark swallowed, nodding as he did. "I talked to him in Paris on Thursday, as a matter of fact. He said he would be over again at Christmas. Or earlier, if we needed him."

Sarah found herself watching him eat, remembering all the meals they had shared on the freighter and at the islands they had visited. "Need him for what?" she asked, worry knitting her brow. Were the two men on another case together?

Mark reached into his shirt pocket and pulled out a folded piece of paper. He handed it to Sarah. "Here. Read this."

She opened it, trying to disguise the shaking of her hands as she did. She started reading.

Dear Sarah

 O R X Y O A
L E X E Y L
I A L V M I
O S R W E U
Y E L U P M

Mark

"A cryptogram," she exclaimed, her eyes lighting up. She loved solving puzzles. "Since it's a five-by-six matrix, I'll assume the original message was written in that form for ciphering."

Mark flashed her an amused glance as he spread jelly over his toast after finishing the omelet.

"From the abundance of vowels and absence of unusual letters, I'll assume it's a simple transposition rather than substitution, and that it's in regular English rather than some secret language." She smiled over at Mark. "You know I'm not good at languages."

He scowled at her. "What do you mean—simple?" he demanded. "There's nothing simple about either the cryptogram or the original message. It took me a week to figure out how to write it."

"Oh," she said meekly. "One of the most common transpositions is an orderly sequence. Umm, maybe a spiral. I need a probable word to start it. Here're two sets of *Y-O* and two *U*'s. And here's an *L-O*. There's one *V*."

Mark was clearly chagrined. "That isn't *Y-O* and *L-O*. It's *O-Y* and *O-L*."

"I pay no attention to the actual order when I'm getting started," she explained. "So, assuming the *O-L-I* in the first column of the cryptogram is the first row in the message, it would read *I-L-O*." She grabbed a pencil and wrote this down neatly.

He crunched on the toast, then licked his fingers, and

wiped his mouth on the napkin when he finished the meal. "So what's next, smarty?"

Her glance was apologetic. "I think I have it figured out. You wrote in a spiral starting in the middle of the first row and moving in a counterclockwise direction." She wrote the message on the bottom of the note in matrix form.

```
I L O V E Y
O U W I L L
Y O U M A R
R Y M E P L
E A S E X X
```

She read it to him. "I love you. Will you marry me, please? Kiss. Kiss."

He grabbed the note. "I didn't say kiss-kiss," he denied.

"You used two *X*'s to fill out the matrix." She kept her eyes on the counter in front of her. "In love notes, *X*'s mean kisses."

"I'd rather deliver mine in person," he murmured, leaning close to her.

She moved from his compelling presence, getting up and taking her coffee into the living room. "Are you and Michael on another case?" she asked when he followed her and they were both seated, one on each side of the coffee table.

"No." Mark's face was puzzled as he looked at her. Why was she withdrawing? Had he misread her actions when he arrived? "He said he would be my best man if I wanted him. I thought your friend, Jennifer Westlake, could stand up for you. We could ask Dr. Fielding to give you away, if you like." He waited through an interminable silence, watching as an expression of agony passed across her face. She was trying to tell him she didn't want him, he thought. There was a sinking sensation in his chest. "Sarah?" he questioned softly.

She twisted her hands together. "We don't have to get married," she told him earnestly. "If you want to come and see me when you're in this area, that would be okay." A tide of blood rushed up her face as she realized how *available* she sounded.

A smile twitched at the corners of his mouth as he visibly relaxed. He waved a negligent hand. "Oh, I think marriage would be best. With my memory for faces and yours for facts, I don't think we should let those traits be lost to the genetic pool, do you?" He leaned forward, forearms resting on his knees, and gave her a serious stare.

"Well, no," she agreed, flustered by his intent gaze.

"Oh, Sarah." He laughed softly. Rising from his chair, he came to her, lifting her easily and setting her on his lap after taking her place.

She laid a hand on his shoulder, holding herself away from him. "Mark, think! If we marry, your life will be restricted. You won't be able to take a vacation without letting the State Department know every single thing you're going to do."

He pulled her close and nuzzled her ear. "I don't care if they know I'm going to make love to you every night."

"You have an exciting career," she continued. "You're used to a life of adventure."

He lifted his head. "No, most of my work is routine, just like anyone's gets to be. The real adventure started when I met you."

For a long minute, they looked at each other, her eyes questioning while his answered.

"I've resigned, darling," he said quietly. "That life hasn't satisfied me in a long time. Until I met you, I didn't know what I was looking for. Now, if you wouldn't mind supporting me for a while, I have a plan. Can you afford to keep a man?" he teased.

"I only have to sigh and gaze out the window of my office with longing, and they give me a raise and a bigger room," she bragged.

They laughed together.

"What a lovely thing freedom is," he reflected. "The freedom to laugh together . . . to love."

"Yes," she whispered, suddenly knowing that all the bitter ghosts of his past were exorcised and that they really did have a future.

He lifted her hand to his lips, then stood, letting her feet slip down to the floor. Keeping her hand in his, he went toward her bedroom. "I'd like to go back to school and get my doctorate."

"Doctorate?" she asked.

"Yes, in Political Science. I got my master's degree in Paris."

"Oh, yes. The widow," she muttered.

He lifted her downcast chin. "You have no worries, my love. There's no one in my heart but you."

"Nor mine. I love you." Her grin wobbled, then disappeared.

With a sure stride, he guided her into the room, stopping beside her bed. With calm fingers, he began to undress her. His head dipped to her breasts as soon as he had them uncovered. "Small but perfectly luscious," he judged them. "I've dreamed of this many times since we last made love." He wanted to kiss her all over, but he didn't think she had enough experience for that yet. He would be patient, teaching her the arts of love slowly. He stripped her then himself completely. They lay down together.

"What happened to everyone?" she asked, stroking his cheek with loving fingers. "The papers said Baruch would be brought back here for trial."

"Yes, that's right. The others will be tried under Greek law."

She looked sad. "I liked Jori. He seemed friendly."

Mark groaned. "What a mind you have! Here I am, half out of my senses with wanting you after all these weeks, and you're thinking of another man, several of them, in fact." Gently he teased her out of her mood and away from thoughts of the past.

Her lips stopped any other complaints as she leaned over and kissed him thoroughly. Her hands rubbed down his sides, across his thighs, and back up his abdomen until his breath threatened to vacate his lungs permanently. He caught her hands and held them in his.

Rolling over her, he gazed possessively into her face, where he saw the glow of passion flaming higher and higher. His lips went to her throat, and he kissed and tasted her there before moving on.

Sarah began to feel heated and breathless as her lover showered her with the living proof of his desire for her. Fires ignited in all the places that he caressed, and she felt the magic returning, flooding over her like a sea in a raging storm. The nearness of this man created a tide of longing in her. "Mark," she pleaded.

He raised himself slightly from her, his eyes pausing on the scar on her arm.

"It's only a scar," she began.

"I know," he said, smiling into her eyes, letting her see all the way into his soul. Bending to her breasts, he kissed one, then the other, and whispered, "Land of milk and honey." He caressed each full, succulent tip with his tongue until she was restless with passion.

Sarah knew a complete happiness like none other in her life. This man loved her, all of her, for all the things she meant to him. And she loved him in just the same way. She stroked his shoulders, his arms and back—all the warm, sheltering strength of him.

Mark let his passion go as he kissed and tasted each part of her, knowing there was nothing she wouldn't accept from him and from his love. He kissed her everywhere and gave free reign to all his senses in enjoying her. When her cries urged him to completion, he rose over her and joined them into one whole, perfect being.

Looking down into her radiant face, he felt his heart expand to fill his chest, his body. "Sarah," he said in passionate tones, "Sarah, my shining joy."

Sarah. Home.

EYE OF THE STORM

MAURA SEGER

A powerful
portrayal of
the events of
World War II in the
Pacific, *Eye of the Storm* is a riveting story of how love
triumphs over hatred. In this, the first of a three book
chronicle, Army nurse Maggie Lawrence meets Marine
Sgt. Anthony Gargano. Despite military regulations
against fraternization, they resolve to face together
whatever lies ahead.... Also known by her fans as
Laurel Winslow, Sara Jennings, Anne MacNeil and
Jenny Bates, Maura Seger, author of this searing novel,
was named by ROMANTIC TIMES as 1984's Most
Versatile Romance Author.

At your favorite bookstore in March.

EYE-B-1

READERS' COMMENTS ON SILHOUETTE DESIRES

"Thank you for Silhouette Desires. They are the best thing that has happened to the bookshelves in a long time."
—V.W.*, Knoxville, TN

"Silhouette Desires—wonderful, fantastic—the best romance around."
—H.T.*, Margate, N.J.

"As a writer as well as a reader of romantic fiction, I found DESIREs most refreshingly realistic—and definitely as magical as the love captured on their pages."
—C.M.*, Silver Lake, N.Y.

"I just wanted to let you know how very much I enjoy your Silhouette Desire books. I read other romances, and I must say your books rate up at the top of the list."
—C.N.*, Anaheim, CA

"Desires are number one. I especially enjoy the endings because they just don't leave you with a kiss or embrace; they finish the story. Thank you for giving me such reading pleasure."
—M.S.*, Sandford, FL

*names available on request